Pie – Eyed

A Pieface O'Riley Recipe for Murder

by
E Penniman James

ISBN: 9798873361359

for
Buster & Iris

The following is a work of fiction. Any similarities to actual people, places, or events, unless deliberately expressed otherwise by the author are purely coincidental.

1

Pieface O'Riley was at it again.

"Get down from there, you dang cat. That's a thousand dollars worth of pie!" snapped Zach Mack, along with a kitchen towel, and a black blur went flying off the countertop.

"What's the matter, Zach?" Jaq Mack inquired as she came down the stairs wearing nothing but a towel, combing her long blond hair, "Is Pieface at it again?"

"He sure is," Zach replied, "and one of these days he going to get his whiskers plucked if he doesn't keep his paws of my pies!"

"C'mon, Zach, relax. He can't resist. We didn't call him Pieface for nothing, you know."

"It'll be kitten pot pie if he doesn't learn to stay out of the kitchen when I'm baking."

"Pieface is just like you – he'll never learn."

Zachary Mack was every inch a pieman. He stood 6'3" in bare feet and weighed 267 pounds soaking wet, which he often was when he emerged from the baking chamber, as he liked to refer to it, cradling a fresh, hot pie in his oven mitts. His tousled brown hair hung to the collar of his hand-tailored dress shirt, always appointed with vintage Jerry Garcia tie. His taste in cravats was a constant bone of contention with his wife Jacqueline, a stunning woman of 5'10" whose slender physique was made even more attractive when set beside her husband's ample frame.

"What is it with those ties?" Jaq would complain. "They're not only out of fashion, their only purpose was to keep some rockstar full of Persian heroin. And who ever heard of a baker in a tie?"

"My dear Jaq," would be Zach's calm reply, "I am not 'a baker'. I am Zach Mack, Piemaker to the Stars, and it is necessary that my working attire reflect my status. Hence the neckwear. As for rockstars and heroin, I wouldn't be where I am today without them."

Jaq paused at the foot of the stairs. "What are you making? It smells divine."

"It's a new turn on cocoanut custard. Should be pretty good."

"Of course it will be good. After all, it's the latest creation of Zach Mack, Piemaker to the Stars."

Zach had started out working for Fabulous Foods, a catering business in New York. The primary clientele were musicians, and to say they had a taste for the unusual was putting it mildly. Cocaine cupcakes, Quaalude soufflé, and bezendrine biscuits were Zach's specialties, and the clients ate them up. It was his Opium Pudding Pie that was Zach's big break. Baked in a chocolate-crumb crust, filled with opium-laced vanilla pudding and topped with whipped cream, it was pie on which you could truly OD. Keith Richards actually did, eating two in one sitting. Zach was soon established as New York's premier piemaker with a list of upper-crust clientele from the entertainment fields. The Mullholland Drive crowd loved his wares as much as the rockers, so expanding to Hollywood, Zach started Bi-Costal Baking.

Jaq pulled her tortoise-shell comb through her long blond hair. "Who's it for?"

9

"Daisy MacDailey."

"Cocoanut for Daisy? I thought she was more the prune type."

"Very funny. In fact, the Perfect Prune Parfait Pie was concocted in her honor. This pie, however, is a treat for the cast and crew of that new Off-Off Broadway troupe that Daisy is promoting."

"Oh yeah, I remember you talking about them. What's their name – The Clam Girls?"

"Please. It's The Marxist Sisters."

"That's right – the radical lesbian theatrical commune. Don't they live in some abandoned schoolhouse in Williamsburg?"

"Williamsburg? How twentieth century. No, they live in an abandoned tile factory in Bushwick. They call it the Courtyard Playhouse. Go figure. Bushwick . . . no place for the Piemaker to the Stars to be plying his wares."

"That's what you said when we moved to Park Slope, and things have turned out pretty well."

It was in Beverley Hills, at a party for Robert Downey, Jr., where Zach met Jacqueline Jillison. Her waist-length blond hair and deep blue eyes inspired Zach to create Jaq's Blueberry Hill Pie. She took one bite and said, "I've found my thrill. Marry me, you fool." Zach was a fool, of course, but not such a one as to pass up an offer like that. At Jaq's urging, they relocated to Brooklyn. Zach's new enterprise, The Pie Galaxy, opened at 787 President Street in the leafy neighborhood of Park Slope. Jaq took over the promotional end of the business while Zach busied himself whipping up new confections of eggs, butter, sugar, flour and drugs. Everything was

10

smooth sailing until one morning when a little black cat appeared outside the front door of the shop.

Zach was busily separating eggs. "Can't argue with you there, my dear. Things have turned out –"

His reply was interrupted by a tremendous clatter. The Macks turned around to discover cocoanut custard all over the kitchen floor. From the middle of the mess, a jet-black furball looked up, licking his paws.

"PIEFACE!"

2

Jaq had finished cleaning up the kitchen floor while Zach polished off what was edible of the remains of his cocoanut custard experiment.

"Not bad, not bad at all. But it needs a few more egg yolks, I think," Zach mused as he wiped his chin.

"More egg yolks? How many did you use?"

"I used 6 eggs, but I think it needs 6 more yolks"

"Jesus, Zach, what are you making - a dessert or a death sentence?"

"Jaq, how many times have I told you? When it comes to baking, the French are right. Butter is good for you-"

"And the egg is the perfect food. I know, I know," Jaq broke in, "but this is probably full of cream already, and six eggs ..."

"Who's the piemaker here? And you're not going to eat it. It's for Daisy MacDailey, who you can't stand anyway. What's it to you if she has a coronary?"

"I don't even know Daisy MacDailey. I just can't stand her TV show."

"Same difference. Well, I'm just glad I hadn't glazed it before Pieface got his nose into it."

"Glazed?"

"Yes. I'm going to burn a sugar crust on it, like crème brulee." Zach opened a drawer, pulling out a ziplock bag containing a pearlescent white lump the size of a spaldeen. "Except . . ."

"Except it's a sugar/coke glaze."

"Exactly"

"I should have known Daisy would go for the blow."

"Well, she is a blowhard after all. Still, it numbs your palate. Seems like a waste of good pie to me."

"Seems like a waste of good coke to me."

"It is good. 100% pure Peruvian flake. Want some?" Zach scraped a little off the spaldeen with a measuring spoon.

"Why not? After all, what's good for the pie . . ."

"Is good for the piemaker. And the piemaker's wife as well. After you, my dear."

Jaq and Zach had their taste, then Zach cracked some eggs and began separating the yolks.

"Mmm, that is nice," Jaq said with a little smile. "Maybe you're on to something here. Coca-for-Cocoanuts Custard Cream pie. But what got Daisy off the prunes?"

"I told you, this is for that theater company. They're doing a revival of 'The Cocoanuts', and Daisy wanted something special for the opening night party."

"'The Cocoanuts'? Never heard of it."

"You're so young, my dear. 'The Cocoanuts' was the Marx Brothers first film."

"Oh, I get it – the Marxist Sisters do the Marx Brothers. What's up with the theater these days? Everything seems to be a stage version of some old movie."

13

"Well, this is actually a stage version of a movie version of the original stage version."

"Sounds like a third generation Xerox."

"You don't even know what a Xerox is. Anyway, the final dress rehearsal is tomorrow night and we're invited."

"To go to Williamsburg? No, thank you."

"It's Bushwick, baby, and you're going. The Mayor will be there."

"Mayor Mike? I'd better go pick out my dress."

"And take that dang cat with you. At a grand a pie, I can't have him sticking his nose into another one."

"Don't you talk about Pieface like that." Jaq scooped up the fuzzy blackness and headed for the stairs. "You know we couldn't live without him."

"Hmm," Zach replied as he measured out flour for a new crust, "Hmm."

THE MARXIST SISTERS' COCA-FOR-COCOANUTS
CUSTARD CREAM PIE

For the crust
        ½ cup bleached flour
        dash salt
        ½ cup fresh shredded cocoanut
        cocoanut milk
For the filling
        1 cup superfine sugar
        ¼ tsp salt
        6 eggs
        6 egg yolks
        1 cup heavy cream
        1½ cup fresh shredded cocoanut
        ½ cup cocoanut milk
        ¼ cup butter
        !½ tsp vanilla
        1 tbsp Mount Gay Rum
For the topping
        ½ cup sugar
        3.5 grams cocaine

Crust – Combine flour and salt. Using a pastry comb, cut flour mixture into cocoanut. Gradually add cocoanut milk to obtain a workable dough. Roll out and place in deepdish pie pan. Line with parchment paper, weight crust with baker's weight. Cook 6 minutes in 450' oven. Remove weight and paper, cook 5 minutes more till golden. Cool on wire rack.

Filling – Combine sugar and salt in sauce pan. Slowly whisk in cocoanut milk and cream. Cook over low heat till bubbly, then lower heat and cook 2 minutes more, whisking constantly. Remove from heat. Gently beat eggs and yolks to blend. Pour eggs into hot mixture in a slow steady stream while mixing with a spatula. Return to low heat, bring mixture just below boil, then cook 2 minutes, whisking constantly. Do not allow mixture to boil. Remove from heat; stir in butter, vanilla and rum. Pour mixture into baked shell and refrigerate overnight.

Topping – Combine sugar and cocaine. Sprinkle topping evenly over custard. Cook under broiler or using propane torch till topping browns. Chill well.

Serves 2-8

3

Daisy MacDailey was frantic. The forehead beneath her bottle-blond Prince Valiant-cum-pageboy hairdo was the color of a Jersey raspberry in a June heatwave. She was screaming into her iPhone at the top of her lungs.

"Whaddya mean, the caterer died! Just like a man, you can never depend on them. Whaddam I gonna do? You know the Mayor. He eats like a horse! A pig is more like it. Actually, he eats like a horse that thinks it's a pig!"

Daisy's assistant could be heard mumbling some reply.

"Jesus Fucking Christ! What do I pay you for, to look pretty? Well, that's part of what I pay you for, but that's not all. Gimme an idea, any idea! We've only got a few . . . Mack? That overpriced piece of shit! I'm already paying him a thousand bills for one goddam lousy pie, and it's cocoanut! That's not gonna do! The Mayor is on a high-protein diet! He's gonna want some real fuckin' food, you nitwit!"

More mumbling.

"Waddya mean, savory? Mack's a piemaker, you dumbshit! You know, peach, apple. What are we gonna serve, fucking mincemeat? You'll be mincemeat in a minute if you don't come up with something!"

Daisy threw her iPhone across the room. It bounced off the walnut paneling of the office wall and exploded into bits.

"Fucking cheap piece of shit! I paid a thousand bucks for this frikkin' thing and it doesn't even bounce off the wall – motherfucker!"

Planted behind her desk like a Venus Flytrap, Daisy was turning a lovely shade of scarlet. There was a gentle rap on the door.

"Get in here, you! And how many times do I have to tell you, if you're gonna knock on my office door, knock on it! You sound like some little timmy dude knockin' on the door of a bathroom stall in the Minneapolis airport, for Christ's sake!"

Constance Carruthers, who was brunette and quite pretty, peeked around the edge of the office door she had opened a crack. "Sorry to disturb you, Ms. MacDailey, I tried your phone, but ..."

"My fucking phone is fucking broken thank you very fucking much. Now, I'm gonna have to shell out another grand to get a new one!"

"Excuse me, Ms. MacDailey, but the prices have dropped – plus you get a new phone every year at no cost."

"Cocksuckers! Charge me a grand, then sell 'em to the little people for chump change! I thought I was getting something exclusive, goddam it! Order me a new one right away and have them send it over toot-fucking-sweet! Now, whadda we gonna feed the asshole mayor?"

Constance steadied herself, tightly grasping her daily calendar. She tugged on the hem of her taupe jacket and smoothed the skirt of her conservative outfit, then gently cleared her throat. She had been Daisy MacDailey's personal assistant for ten years, but she had never quite gotten used to dealing with Daisy's temper. She took another breath, then quietly said, "I've spoken with Mr. Mack."

"You've spoken with Mr. Mack, have you? Well, what does that overweight pissant pastry pusher have to say?" Daisy roared.

17

"Well, he says it's short notice, but he could whip something up today if necessary."

"Whip something up? Whip something up? I'll take a bullwhip to him, flay him, and serve him to the fuckin' mayor! What does he propose?"

"A bean pie."

Daisy Mac Dailey was dumfounded. She'd heard some harebrained schemes before, but this one took the cake. Examining the yellow nails of her plump, pink fingers, Daisy spoke in a very soft voice. "A bean pie. Zack Mack, Piemaker to the Stars, wants me to serve the Mayor a bean pie. A bean pie."

There was an uncomfortable silence. Constance Carruthers shifted her weight slightly from leg to leg. The silence continued.

"What should I tell him?" Constance finally managed to squeeze out.

"I'll tell you what to tell him!" Daisy's neck now resembled the star attraction of a Maine lobsterbake. "You tell him to make that fucking bean pie right now and that it had better be the best goddam fucking bean pie anyone has every tasted or I'll have his dick on a stick and we'll show the Mayor what a weenie roast really looks like! Now get out of my office!"

"Yes, Ms. MacDailey, right away." Constance said as she backed out of the room.

"AND GET ME MY NEW PHONE PRONTO, BIRDWASTE! AND A GODDAM GEEK TO PROGRAM IT. AND I WANT A CHEESEBURGER AND DOUBLE ORDER OF FRIES RIGHT NOW! I SAID NOW, DAMMIT!"

18

"Yes, Ms. MacDailey" Constance closed the door as quietly as she could.

Then she went to her desk, sat down, pulled a bottle of pills from her purse and swallowed four Lorazepam tablets without water.

4

Zach was stirring the pot when his phone rang.

"Oh, hi CC," Zach said as he set down his spoon. "Actually, I'm working on it right now . . . I could tell from our conversation earlier that Daisy would want to go ahead with it, and the beans take a little time . . . Hey, you get down from there!" Pieface had crept on to the counter and was licking sauce off the spoon. "No, not you, CC, my cat. He has a knack for getting into the middle of things. Anyway, it'll be ready for tonight . . . Of course he'll like it. I'm making it, right? . . . Of course there will be no pork . . . OK, that sounds fine . . . See you at seven."

Zach slipped his phone into the pocket of his apron and turned back to the beans.

"If you don't get your nose out of that pan, I'm going to put you in there. CC said no pork; she didn't mention anything about no felines."

Pieface straightened his tail and gave Zach a look of supreme indifference, turned from the pot and began nosing around the spicerack.

"Let's see, the molasses is in, a touch of mace, some cumin . . . what else do we need here?"

Pieface, pawing at the jars, managed to knock one over, covering the counter with small oblong pills.

"Pieface, you're a genius! The secret ingredient I was looking for – Xanax. Just what we need for Mayor Mike's Chill Pill Bean Pie. No, don't worry, they won't know – I'm not going to go overboard. Judicious use of spices is the hallmark of fine baking. Hmm, these are 2 mg, so a dozen should be about right."

Zach counted out 13 pills, putting the rest back in the bottle. The pills went into the spice grinder. "That's why they call it a baker's dozen," Zach said to the cat, slipping one under his tongue. "Don't you start getting any ideas, Pieface. The last thing I need is a looped pussycat." Then, with a flourish, Zach twisted the grinder over the pan of beans.

"Perfect. Now let's put these babies in the oven for a while. We're going to have fun tonight, Pieface. I have a feeling that everyone will just love the performance."

Snapping his tail on the counter, the black cat lifted his head and came out with a sound something like "Mer-ee-owll"

"My thoughts exactly," Zach replied as he reached for the lard.

5

The office of the Honorable Michael Hindenberg, Mayor of the City of New York, was a marvel of modern technology. Referred to as 'the bullpen', it more closely resembled a beehive, with the focus of all activity on the queen bee. The Mayor's desk sat in the center of a large open room. The desktop was empty except for a computer screen. There was a clear space about four feet wide surrounding the desk, then rings of smaller and increasingly more cluttered desks, all garnished with multiple computer screens, radiating around it. The Mayor would sit in front of the screen and gesture. No keyboards, no voice commands, the screen would respond to the movements of the Mayor's hand. Waving his palm, a greenpath would appear along the Brooklyn Heights waterfront. This image would then immediately appear on all the screens on all the other desks in the office. Deputy mayors would then begin determining locations for the highrise condominiums that would overlook the new park. Snapping his fingers, bike paths would appear on all the busy commercial streets and avenues of the city. More deputy mayors would begin drafting press releases about the Mayor's commitment to the environment, while still more deputy mayors would begin processing the paperwork authorizing hiring of the new traffic officers who would be giving out tickets for blocking bike lanes to all the delivery trucks supplying the local businesses. Clapping his hands twice, a daffodil might appear on the screen. Instantly, assistant deputy mayors would begin drafting proclamations declaring the daffodil the official flower of the City of New York, while sub-assistant deputy mayors would authorize budgetary expenditures supplying free daffodils to the cities trendiest and most rapidly gentrifying neighborhoods. All in all, it was a spectacle that would bring tears to the eyes of efficiency experts, autocrats and the few remaining longtime residents of the City of New York. Today, however, bringing New York City into the 21ˢᵗ century was not the order of business. The Marxist Sisters were on the calendar today.

"I have to go to Bushwick tonight? I have to go to Bushwick tonight? Who set this up? Can't someone from Cultural Affairs handle this?" The pinched adenoidal tone of the Mayor's voice brought all activity in the office to a standstill. "Don't tell me there's only two staff people left in the department. I know that very well. It is my sworn duty to operate this city in the most cost-effective manner possible. By eliminating redundant bureaucracy and institutional dependency, I've opened the way for the private sector to step up into the supporting role it has always been destined play. Don't tell me corporate funding for the arts has fallen. That's certainly not the case at Hindenberg LLC. Now what about this Bushwick thing? I hate Brooklyn. Except for Fourth Avenue. With all those twelve story buildings, the expansive boulevard, complete with landscaped center islands, it's beautiful. Once they get that 19-story tower up and cover that eyesore subway tunnel. And talk about revenue generation! All we need is for DOT to figure out where all those 18-wheelers will go. I promised Daisy MacDailey I would go to Bushwick? I can't believe it. Even before I stopped drinking, I would never do such a stupid thing. Oh, that's right. The Marxist Sisters. The Courtyard Playhouse. Revitalizing the neighborhood with the help of local artists so we can drive the low rent losers out and start converting everything to co-ops and condos. Well, there had better be food. What's that? Daisy called to say that Zach

23

Mack is making a pie in my honor for the event? Well, that's a horse of a different color. They don't call him the Piemaker to the Stars for nothing. As long as I don't have to stay to see the show. I hate the theater. All those people talking. Important issues being discussed. They should just listen to me, forget about all this other nonsense, then go home and watch Dancing with the Goons. Now, that's entertainment. No, absolutely not. I don't care if I'm the Green Mayor, I am not riding on the J train. OK,OK, here's what we do. Drive me in the Suburban to the Marcy Avenue Station. I'll get on the train there and get off at Flushing – that's only a couple stops. Have the press at Flushing, it's a photo op, Mayor visits the city's new artistic frontier, takes mass transit to the outer boroughs, etc. Under no circumstances will I stay any later than 8 o'clock."

6

Comrade Sioban Koslowski woke late that morning. From the upper berth of the bunkbed she shared with the props comrade, she looked across the dormitory to the grimy window facing the elevated tracks of the J and Z line. The low rumble of the passing train had shaken her out of her late morning slumbers. She thought about how lucky she was not to have to sleep in the bed next to the window. Here, the grinding of the wheels on the tracks was not so noticeable, and you could hardly hear the window rattling at all. Sioban, or Comrade Shy as all the comrades called her, sat up and stretched, running her hands through her close-cropped red hair. She had already missed mandatory yoga at dawn on the factory roof, which meant she would be put on toilet duty for a week, but she didn't care. This morning Sioban was extraordinarily happy, even with a week's worth of bowl swabbing staring her in the face. Tonight was the final dress rehearsal of The Marxists Sisters production of 'The Cocoanuts'. Sioban actually pinched herself at the thought. Here she was, just three months out of Sarah Lawrence, and she was the dramaturge of one of New York City's most important Off-Off Broadway companies! Tomorrow, the show would open, there would be a review in Time Out, and her life-long dream would have come true. Granted, her position was unpaid, she was required to share living quarters with 15 other women, had to travel to Williamsburg to be able to take a shower at the Metropolitan Pool, attend rehearsals eight hours a day, spend four hours going over director's notes and revising the script, and then perform menial chores around the factory that served as the company's home, but still, she was excited. More than

25

excited, thrilled! "Of course, there are sacrifices," Shy thought to herself, "but I'm doing it. I'm really working in the New York theater!" Her reverie was interrupted by a gruff voice.

"Comrade Koslowski, are you still in bed? Get your ass out of there. We've got a meeting with Comrade Mildow in ten minutes." It was the stage manager. Her name, as it appeared in the program was 'S. Shurtz'. No one knew what the S. stood for. The comrades called her 'Shurtzy' or 'Comrade Shurtz', depending on their position in the company.

"Sorry, Comrade Shurtz, we were so late last night going over notes, I just couldn't get up at dawn today. I want to be fresh for tonight's final dress." Shy was trying to find a way to climb out of her bunk in a somewhat dignified matter. It wasn't easy, considering she was almost six feet tall with wide hips and a full bosom. Shurtz stood there staring at her as she hoisted one leg over the bed rail to the ladder.

"Panties and a T-shirt. What's the matter with you? You should sleep naked like the rest of the comrades," Shurtz barked.

"I'm sorry, Ms. Shurtz, I was just so tired when I went to bed last night, I just collapsed."

"Don't give me that crap. You managed to get your pants off. Or did someone else do that? Listen here, Comrade, it's your revolutionary duty to sleep in the raw. Pyjamas or anything like them are bourgeois decadence. Now get it in gear," Shurtz snapped as she left the room.

26

Her bare feet feeling the cold of the concrete floor, standing in the dorm in her underwear, Comrade Sioban Koslowski pinched herself once more. Dress rehearsal tonight, tomorrow – we open!

7

S. Shurtz was a stage manager's stage manager. She ran a tight ship. She was always fifteen minutes early for rehearsal, made sure the furniture and props required were readily available, brooked no nonsense from the cast and never contradicted the director. Shurtz made sure rehearsal started on time, observed the union-mandated breaks, and finished promptly. She noted the movements of the actors with precise detail in the production book, as well as any changes to the script, and made sure the actors heard about it if they deviated from the proscribed action. Built like a jonnypump and dressed in her standard outfit of brown plaid short sleeve shirt, khaki shorts, crew socks and topsiders, her salt and pepper hair parted on the left, S. Shurtz walked into the classroom The Marxist Sisters used for production meetings. Everything was in its proper place, but S. Shurtz was not. This morning, S. Shurtz was agitated. She thought back over the years she had spent as a comrade. In fact, S. Shurtz was a founding member of The Marxist Sisters. It was Shurtz who had found the tile factory, convinced the city to sell in to The Sisters, cleaned all four stories of decades of debris and squatters. S. Shurtz lived and breathed for The Marxist Sisters, and she dedicated herself to the revolutionary goal The Sisters were fighting for - socially progressive, feminist theatrical presentations, with music. But today, S. Shurtz was agitated.

"It's that damn dramaturge," she thought to herself as she set out seven freshly sharpened No. 2 pencils for Teena Mildow, artistic director of The Marxist Sisters. "I bet she's even had sex with a man. How bourgeois."

S. Shurtz's cogitations were interrupted as Teena and Shy entered the class-room. Shy had pulled on a pair of grey sweatpants, but was still wearing the T-shirt she had slept in last night. In a word, Comrade Shy looked fuzzy. Teena Mildow, on the other hand, was the kind of woman who liked to look sharp. From her razorcut raven hair, her thin rectangular black glasses that highlighted her hazel eyes while resting on her sharp, sculptured nose, her sharp smile that showed her slightly less sharp teeth, her sharp, shapely breasts that poked up beneath her black, French-cut t-top, to the sharply pointed toes of her black leather boots which reached just below her knees, heels clicking on the tile floor as she walked, Teena Mildow looked sharp.

"Good morning, Shurtzy. Looks like you're ready to go, as usual," Teena said in her clear, cheerful voice.

"Just doing my duty, Comrade Mildow," was Shurtz's curt reply.

"Your professionalism is always appreciated. Let's get to work."

The three women sat at a table, Teena on one side facing Shurtz and Shy. They took out notebooks. Teena picked up one of the pencils and tried balancing it on her fingertip.

"I don't want to belabor anything today. I was happy with last night's run-through. Shurtz, you got my notes on the costumes and lights last night. That's your priority today. Shy, I'm very happy with the book. You've done a great job, especially for a young woman fresh out of school. All those hours we spent together comparing the screenplay with the stage version have really paid off. We've maximized the dia-lectic of the class struggle without sacrificing any laughs. I've got to meet with the cast now, so unless there's anything . . ."

29

"There is one thing, Comrade Mildow." Shurtz's voice was as chilly as Mick Jagger's handshake. "There was a line fluff last night, pretty serious. I've already talked to Teri about it, but I thought I'd bring it to your attention as well."

"Are you talking about the top of Act Two? Shy and I changed that line two nights ago. Shy's idea, actually. Much funnier now. I thought I'd gone over that with you."

"I don't recall getting any notes on a script change. It's Comrade Koslowski's responsibility to communicate all textual-"

Teena interrupted. "I said I didn't want to belabor anything. I'm sure I talked with you about the change, and if Shy forgot to speak with you-"

"Comrade Koslowski has her duties and she should take them seriously. It's for the good of the revolution."

"I know, Shurtzy, I know. But I don't think this one little error is going to stop the revolution. Now, I'm going to meet the cast. Shurtzy, go talk with the designers. Shy, you come with me."

"Yes, Comrade Mildow." Shy quickly stood and waited deferentially for the director.

"That Comrade stuff gets a little thick sometimes. You can call me Teena – I'd like that."

"If you say so, Teena."

"I do say so, and I'm the director. Now, let's go." Teena draped a slim arm around Shy's more substantial shoulders. "You must be excited, Shy. I mean, your first show in New York and all."

"I'm just excited to be working with such a talented artist as you, Comrade – I mean, Teena"

"What a sweet thing to say," Teena replied, giving Shy a peck on the cheek. "Look at you, turning all rosy!"

Teena squeezed Shy's neck gently, then led her out the door. "Did you hear that Daisy has ordered a Zach Mack pie for the opening party? His pies are to die for – I can't wait! Oh, Shurtzy, bring my pencils, please," Teena called out as her heels clicked down the hall.

S. Shurtz rose from her chair and collected the sharpened pencils one by one. Then she left the classroom, putting out the lights behind her.

8

Jaq could see Pieface in the mirror of her vanity as she was putting on her sapphire earrings. The black cat was watching her, too. Crouched on the king-size bed in the Mack's bedroom, his greenish-yellow eyes were zeroed in on the shiny blue jewels.

"Hey, you, what are you looking at?" Jaq asked as she flipped her hair over her shoulder. "You already ate my rubies. Don't start dreaming about these."

"Mer-ee-owll"

"I know, I know. Butter wouldn't melt in your mouth. That's what you said the day you showed up at the Pie Galaxy."

*

Jaq loved to remember that morning. Bright summer sun, the steaminess of August not yet rising to a boil, she had been walking up President Street when she noticed a black splotch on the Galaxy's bright green door. "What could that be? We just painted the door last week," Jaq was wondering to herself when, as she opened the wrought iron gate, the black splotch took off in a mad dash down the block. "Poor kitty!" Jaq cried. "Come back, I won't hurt you." But the cat was gone. Closing the door as she stepped inside the Galaxy, Jaq went about her daily routine, flipping on lights, arranging menus, then heading to the office to open the safe. As she came back into the showroom with the register till, Jaq heard the tinkling of the temple bells that hung from the inside knob of the front door.

"I'll be right with you," she said as she walked out of the office, but she found the showroom empty. "That's odd," Jaq said to herself as she slipped the till into the register, "I'm sure I heard the door bell, but the door's closed and there's no one here. I must be losing it." She was heading back to the office when from nowhere came the sound.

"Mer-ee-owll"

"Who's there?" Jaq turned quickly, but saw nothing.

"Mer-ee-owll"

"Show yourself."

And as if responding to Jaq's demand, a small black cat with greenish-yellow eyes and a bright red tongue suddenly jumped onto the counter next to the cash register.

"How did you get in here? I know I closed the door when I came in. You're too little to reach the knob."

"Mer-ee-owll" the cat calmly replied.

"That's your story and you're sticking to it, eh? Come on now, you've got to go. The Health Department will close us down if they find you here." And with that, Jaq chased the cat down from the counter and over to the door. "Hey, move it, you little scootch." Jaq nudged the cat gently with her foot as she opened the shop door, the temple bells jangling. "Out you go."

The cat looked at Jaq, squinted and seemed about to protest this treatment, then suddenly darted out the open door.

"Bye-bye, kiddo. Don't go running in front of any buses."

33

Jaq was in the office putting on her apron when the bells chimed. "Be right there!" she said, adding to herself, "Busy this morning." But when she entered the showroom, once again she found it empty. "Too weird – I'm sure I heard the bells." She leaned down to check on the pie boxes under the counter when she heard a definite 'plop' on the counter top. Raising her head slightly, she came eye-to-eye with the black cat.

"Mer-ee-owll"

"You again! You are quite a sneak. This time I know I shut the door. Well, I don't care, you've got to go." Jaq went to pick up the cat, who quickly jumped onto her left shoulder. "Get down from there. You'll mess up my hair." The doorbells rang again, and this time it was Zach, who practically filled the doorframe as he entered the shop.

"Good morning, Zach. Wait till I tell you the story of this cat."

"What cat?"

"This black cat here on my shoulder."

"There's no black cat on your shoulder."

"What, but just a minute ago . . ." Jaq reached for her left shoulder, but Zach was right – no cat.

"That's the strangest thing! He came through the closed door twice, jumped up on my shoulder, and now he's disappeared!"

"Came through a closed door twice, did he? Then vanished? Didn't even leave a smile behind? Have you been into the pie already this morning, dear?"

"No, I have not and there was a cat in here."

34

"Of course," Zach said smugly as he headed for the office. "I know because that giant rabbit I ran into down the block told me all about it. Now, can we get to work?"

"Don't you dare patronize me, Zachary Mack," Jaq said sharply as she followed him through the office door. "I'm telling you there was a black cat in here."

"Who came through a closed door twice and then disappeared. Yes, I got all that. Now, c'mon. I've got to get started on that ibogaine tart for Al Pacino."

"I'd think you would believe your own wife."

"I do believe you, honey. I just don't believe your cat."

"Hear me now and believe me later, Pieman," Jaq sniffed. As she turned to leave the office, there was a resounding *CRASH* in the showroom.

"What the hell was that?" Zach said as he pushed past Jaq. "I didn't hear the doorbells. What in the world?"

Jaq bumped into Zach, who had stopped in his tracks. He was staring at the floor behind the counter, where four pieplates lay in pieces amidst chunks of cherries, apricots and lemon meringue. Presiding over this disaster was a small black cat with greenish-yellow eyes and a bright red tongue. The cat was cleaning its face with a paw. He lifted his head and fixed Zach in its greenish-yellow gaze.

"Mer-ee-owll"

"Well, aren't you the piefaced devil," Zach said with a tone of respect.

"That's it! He's Pieface O'Reily, the cat who likes dessert! Can we keep him, Zach? He's so cute!"

"Not as cute as me."

35

"No one's as cute as you, Zach, but look at him – he's adorable!"

The black cat, playing with the crust, looked up suddenly, snapping his tail on the floor.

"And he seems to know it, too."

The cat moved its greenish-yellow eyes from Zach to Jaq, then back again.

"Mer-ee-owll"

"Oh, please, Zach, you can tell he likes us."

"More like he knows an easy mark when he sees one. All right, all right, but you've got to take him home. All I need is a Health Inspector to find a cat in here. I'd be busted in a second, and not for Health Code violations."

"I'll take him home right now. C'mere, Pieface."

The black cat leapt into Jaq's arms, then quickly climbed onto her shoulder and started playing with her blonde hair.

"He knows which side his bread is buttered on," Zach said with a snort.

"He's just got his eye on the pie, that's all."

"Well, he certainly knows quality when he sees it."

"You sound jealous, Zach."

"Of a cat? I am Zach Mack, Piemaker to the Stars, and I have the most beautiful wife in the world. Why should I be jealous?"

"Because Pieface and I are going home to cuddle, and you're going to be left all alone in the kitchen."

"An artist find solace in his work. Now, where's that ibogaine?"

*

"Hey, what going on up there with you two?" Zach voice boomed up the stairs, bringing Jaq's attention back to the vanity mirror and her sapphire earring. "We've got to get rolling. I promised CC we'd be there by seven."

"I'll be ready in a sec, as soon as I get the collar and leash on Pieface. Why don't you go get the Pie Wagon? We'll both be ready by the time you get back."

"A cat on a leash. Sheesh."

"Oh, he likes it, Zach. Just like you."

"Not in public."

"Maybe we should try it some time. I'll take you both out for a walk."

"I'm going to get the Pie Wagon before you come up with any more bright ideas. I'll be back in ten minutes."

"We'll be ready for you, big boy," Jaq said, laughing as she slipped the black leather collar around Pieface's neck. "Will you be ready for us?"

9

"Hey, where's my Scotch?"

It was 5:50 as the Mayor was in the rear seat of a black Suburban SUV heading north on Centre Street.

"We removed it, sir. Your orders."

"Don't be ridiculous. I never gave any such order."

"It was a mayoral proclamation, sir. No alcoholic beverages while conducting business by anyone working for the city."

"Since when do I work for the city? You've got things mixed up – the city works for me. We'll have to stop at a liquor store. I'm not going to Bushwick to see Daisy MacDailey without a drink."

"We can stop on St. James, sir."

"No, too obvious. We'll stop after we get across the bridge. Put on the lights and siren."

"Yes, sir." The chauffer pulled out the cherrytop and placed it on the dash as the wailing of the siren began clearing the streets.

"Let's take the Manhattan Bridge. There's that big liquor store on the corner of DeKalb and Ashland – by BAM."

"We'll be there in five minutes, sir. Would you mind buckling your seatbelt?"

"Would you mind working for the Sanitation Department? Now step on it. I'm thirsty."

The Suburban pulled up on DeKalb four and a half minutes later. The Mayor rolled down the black-tinted partition window and handed the chauffer a fifty-dollar bill.

"Get a half-pint of something good . . . make it a pint. Keep the change."

The chauffer returned in a few minutes with a brown paper bag, which he handed to the Mayor. "Macallan? I said something good. This is 10 year old."

"It was the best they had, sir."

"I hate Brooklyn," spat out the Mayor as he cracked the metal seal on the bottle. "Marcy Street station. No siren. I want to drink in peace." The black window slid up silently.

"Yes, sir. What ever you say, sir."

10

It was 6pm when the limo carrying Daisy MacDailey and Constance Carruthers pulled up in front of the Courtyard Playhouse. Constance got out first, followed by the world's biggest, yellowest cashmere car coat.

"Jesus, my knees. I forgot this place was beyond the edge of the earth." Daisy said once she was free from the clutches of the limousine's back seat. "How did they ever find such a fucking dump?" The former tile factory was a squat four-story brown brick structure that occupied the entire block. "Locust and Beaver. There's a sorry-ass address for you. Christ on a bike."

Daisy's real-estate appraisal was cut short by the clicking of bootheels on the ceramic steps of the factory entrance.

"Daisy! I'm so happy you're here, lover! I've been trying to call you all day." Teena Mildow ran with open arms to embrace Daisy, which she almost managed.

"Sorry, honey, Constance broke my fucking phone."

"That doesn't sound like something CC would do." Teena wrapped her arms were around Daisy's neck and started chewing on her earlobe.

"I dropped it in the coffee grinder. It was a very stupid thing for me to do." Constance was worrying the cover of her daily calendar.

"Ruined half a pound of free trade organic Sumatran, at thirty fucking bucks a pound."

"Now, Daisy, I'm sure it was an accident – wasn't it, Connie?"

Constance merely nodded in reply. It made her seem very cool and professional, but the truth was, self-confident women like Teena always made Constance feel insignificant. In fact, almost everyone made Constance feel insignificant. Teena had taken Daisy by the arm and was leading her in the factory door.

"Hey, how come you haven't kissed me yet? Mama's had a rough day, needs some lovin'." Daisy gave Teena a full-on liplock.

"You take my breath away," Teena exclaimed as she regained her balance. "You know, Daisy, this is such an important night. To think that the Mayor will be coming to recognize the achievements of The Marxist Sisters. And it's all because of you."

"It's not me, lover, it's you. You are a great artist Teena, and don't you forget it"

"Flattery will get you everywhere, honey, although you've already been there more than once."

"Oh, I think there's a spot or two I've yet to explore." Daisy smirked as she slapped Teena's rear end.

"I want to introduce you to the company. They're all so excited to finally meet the famous Daisy MacDailey."

"Well, they damn well should be. Come on Constance, quit dragging your ass."

Constance, who had been looking at the trash on the street and wondering if she had ever seen a dirtier sidewalk, put her head down and took several small, quick steps up the factory stairs. "Yes, Ms. MacDailey, sorry, Ms. MacDailey."

41

"Stop with the frikkin apologies already. Jesus Christ."

"Sorry, Ms. MacDailey, I mean yes, Ms. MacDailey."

The three women were headed down a long wide corridor, Teena and Daisy arm in arm, Constance trailing behind. The ceilings and upper walls were a kind of off-white and looked like they hadn't been painted since World War II. Just below waist level, the walls changed color.

"Mucky barf green" Daisy noted. "Lovely."

"Yes, the place could use a paint job, it's true. But for now we're concentrating on the performance space. We've converted the loading dock into a theater-in-the-round. The ceilings are wonderfully high, the sightlines are good and no one is more than eight feet from the stage."

"Isn't that rather close?" Constance interjected.

"In the theater, we refer to it as intimate," replied Teena in her most condescending tone.

"Isn't it rather intimate, then?" Constance asked, summoning all her courage.

"Everything's too intimate for you, you damn biddy. When's the last time anyone got their hands on you, anyway?" Daisy demanded.

"I'm certain I don't understand what you mean, Ms. MacDailey," Constance said as her courage evaporated.

"I believe that. Who'd want to fool around with shriveled stick of celery like you?"

42

"Now, Daisy, be nice. Constance is a very attractive woman." Teena's condescension was dripping down the mucky barf green walls.

"Yeah, well, looks aren't everything. A pulse rate might help."

"Here's the performance space," Teena announced, much to Constance's relief.

The former loading dock looked just like that – a former loading dock. Large gates filled the opposite wall. The floor was pitted and cracked, the ceiling invisible in the darkness overhead. Everything had a fresh coat of flat black paint. Rows of black chairs had been arranged along the walls of the room, leaving the central space open. In the middle of the open area, a single incandescent bulb on a black metal stand was making a feeble attempt at illumination.

"It's fantastic, isn't it? A real black box theater!" Teena gushed.

"Well, it's black, that's for sure," Daisy replied flatly. "What's with that light?"

"The ghost light? It's an old theater tradition. We leave it on overnight."

"Ghost light?" Daisy said with a shudder. "What, somebody fucking die? Turn it off. It gives me the creeps.

"I'll put on the work lights."

Teena wandered off into the shadows. After a moment, there was a click and harsh white light filled the room.

"Where's the scenery?"

Daisy and Teena turned to Constance, who clutched her daily calendar.

43

"What a stupid fucking question. Where's the scenery? You are one dumb bitch." Daisy fumed.

"I'm sorry, Ms. MacDailey."

"Goddamit, I told you to stop apologizing."

"I'm . . . I mean, yes, Ms. MacDailey. I was just wondering aloud … "

"Actually, there is no scenery."

Now it was Daisy and Constance who turned to Teena.

"No scenery?" they asked in unison.

"You see, the purpose of scenery is to create an illusion – the illusion that you are in Florida, for instance, at the site of a building development. But The Marxist Sisters aren't interested in illusion. We are interested in truth. We aim to strip the capitalist illusions of material wealth, personal property, and individual expression bare, reveal them for what they are, lies and distortions whose only purpose is to enslave the proletariat and increase the wealth of the ruling class. Illusions that mislead the people, encouraging them to embrace their alienation, make them active participants in their own enslavement. By removing the bourgeois trapping such as scenery and costumes, The Marxist Sisters aim to rediscover the revolutionary power inherent in all performance."

"You mean, the actresses don't wear any clothes?" Constance asked, gripping her calendar tighter than ever.

"'Actress' is a sexist term, clearly intended to demean the labors of those who are not 'actors'. We refer to the performers as 'actrons'. And they do wear clothes. They don't wear costumes."

44

"What's the difference?"

"Costumes are manifestations of the corrupt class and sexist divisions in capitalist society. Men wear pants, women wear dresses. The rich wear silk, the poor, cotton. The Marxist Sisters reject the artificial social conditioning that costumes perpetrate."

"You mean, you put men in dresses?"

"There are no men in The Marxist Sisters. We are a radical lesbian troupe dedicated to presenting socially progressive, feminist theatrical presentations, with music. The male-dominated capitalist society has perverted the relationship of the sexes. Only by eliminating the male can the female be liberated, and only by liberating the female can the male achieve liberation." Teena explained patiently.

"Oh." Constance was shifting her weight from one leg to the other. "But if they don't wear costumes, what do they wear?"

"Everyone wears gray jumpsuits."

"The entire cast? But how can you tell the difference between the characters?"

"The individuality of the characters is another manifestation of the decadence of the capitalist society," Teena pronounced with an air of finality.

"Oh." Constance buried her nose in her calendar.

"Well, that's got to be the most brilliant thing I've ever heard in my goddam life. Teena, you are a fucking genius! Now let's go meet the cast before the Mayor gets here."

"The dressing rooms are this way." Teena took Daisy's arm again and marched off with the air of a victorious general. Constance took another quick look at the loading dock, empty except for rows of chairs, then hurriedly followed.

11

S. Shurtz strode between the stainless steel tables of the former cafeteria where the ten women who made up the acting company of The Marxist Sisters were seated. The room was silent under the flicker of fluorescent lights. The performers, their hands on the tables in front of them, sat motionless. S. Shurtz continued her march, up one row of tables, down the next. No one turned their head as she passed. The crepe soles of Shurtz's topsiders' made no sound as she walked up and down, back and forth. There was a feeling of a college board entrance exam in the room – everybody sweating bullets while their throats ran dry. Pausing at the head of one of the tables, Shurtz spoke.

"Comrades, our time has almost arrived. Tonight marks the final dress rehearsal for the revolution. By this time tomorrow, the disenfranchised workers of this decadent society will be gathered in our theater, waiting for the match to be struck, the fire to be lit, the call to arms to be raised. And it will be our solemn duty to issue that call, to lead the masses in the glorious revolution that will put an end to the inequity of the capitalist yoke under which we all labor. Take heart, Comrades. Banish all tender thoughts. Steel your hearts and minds, and let every fiber of your being be focused on our goal-"

"Hey, kids, ready to put on a show?" The cheerful tone of Teena Mildow's voice cut through the room like cleaver through a chicken neck. "Everybody happy?"

The cast looked uncertainly at each other, then to the stage manager.

"I believe the cadre is prepared to enter the great struggle." S. Shurtz was still standing at the head of the table.

"Excellent, excellent! Now, everybody, I'm very excited to have the chance to introduce to you the angel of The Marxist Sisters, the women who makes all our work possible, Ms. Daisy MacDailey!"

Daisy and her yellow coat entered the makeshift dressing room. She looked around, smiled widely and was met by total silence.

"On behalf of the cast, I'd like to say what an honor it is to meet you." Shurtz didn't move as she spoke.

"What's going on? Why is everyone so damn quiet?" Daisy asked Teena.

"Discipline, Ms. MacDailey, Discipline." Shurtz remained immobile. "A good production, like a revolution, requires absolute disciple. The Comrades are saving their voices for the work ahead. Engaging in idle chatter would dissipate their energy."

"Everybody seems uptight to me. Whaddya do, shove a stick up their ass or something?"

"Daisy, you crack me up!" Teena said quickly as she saw Schurtz's eyes narrowing. "You're in show biz – you know how important concentration is."

"Yeah, sure, concentration is great, but not as in concentration camp. It's more like Auschwitz than the Great White Way in here."

"The Great White Way. Comrades, see how the euphemisms of this corrupt society reinforce the power structure we are sworn to overthrow." Shurtz balled her hands into fists and leaned forward on the table. "We must crush it, obliterate it, bury it."

"That's right, Shurtzy, but it's final dress. It wouldn't hurt the girls to smile." Teena moved to the head of the table, patting the stage manager on the back.

"You're right, Comrade Mildow, the women can smile if they want."

The company remained motionless with their hands on the tables. Shurtz stared at Daisy. Teena whistled tunelessly.

The door to the cafeteria suddenly swung open. Everyone spun their heads and stared. Constance Carruthers froze like a porcupine stuck on velcro. She opened her mouth, paused, then spoke.

"The Mayor has arrived."

Teena squealed in delight. "The Mayor! Come on, girls, let's go meet him."

The company stood as one and filed silently out the door. Daisy watched for a moment, then turned to Constance.

"What are you lookin' at, dummy? Let's go say hello to Der Hindenberg."

Daisy gave Constance a shove and they headed down the hall, leaving Schurtz alone with the stainless steel tables. She stood there, leaning on her fists. S. Shurtz took a deep breath and walked to the door.

As she shut it behind her, she said, "Just what we need – a man."

12

It was 6:15 when the black Suburban reached the Marcy Street Station. The Mayor rolled down the partition.

"OK, be at the theater in an hour and a half. That'll give me a good excuse for leaving. Don't be late. And take care of this." he said, handing the chauffer the empty Macallan bottle.

Mayor Martin Hindenberg stepped out into the shadows of the elevated tracks. Two large black suits sporting sunglasses and earwires slipped out of the Suburban and followed him up the stairs to the platform. The Mayor climbed the steps smoothly, with only an occasional touch of the handrail to steady him. He opened the emergency exit gate as the suits flashed ID to the token booth clerk. The J was just pulling in to the station. "Tell the conductor we're going express." the Mayor said under his fragrant breath. "What's the hold up?" an elderly Puerto Rican woman cried. The PA barked, "Attention riders, this train is going express, next stop Flushing Avenue. There's another train making all local stops right behind this one." "Let 'em off!" the elderly woman cried again. The Mayor was pushing past people trying to exit. "Get her out of my way!" he snapped. One of the suits grabbed the woman and pulled out a summons book. "I'll catch up." he said to his partner, who slipped through the door as the closing chimes sounded. "Step lively, next stop Flushing Ave," the intercom squealed. The Mayor had squeezed into a seat next to a young Chinese woman and her three children. "I hate Brooklyn" he thought.

At Flushing Avenue, the Mayor left the train and took the elevator to the street. "At least I don't have to use the stairs. I don't know how people do this everyday." The elevator doors opened and lights from the TV cameras blinded him. Photo strobes flashed and reporters clamored.

"Now, come on, let me through. I'm just an average citizen on my way to see some wholesome entertainment. No different than any of the other hard working men and women who make up this great city." The suit had slid beside him. "Make a right, then four blocks. Left on Locust," the suit whispered in the Mayor's ear. The Mayor waved to the press as he moved along the sidewalk. "No questions, please, I'll be making a statement at the theater."

The circus headed down the block, crossing Broadway. As he turned onto Locust Street, the Mayor saw something large and yellow emerge from the Courtyard Playhouse. "Daisy MacDailey – she looks like a Wooly Mammoth that fell into a tub of mustard," he mumbled.

"Right this way, your Honor, so good of you to come!"

"I wouldn't have missed it for the world, Daisy. You know how much I love Bushwick."

"I believe you know my assistant, Constance," Daisy said with and offhand gesture.

"Of course, of course, nice to see you, CC." The Mayor smiled as Constance tugged her jacket and executed a clumsy half-curtsy.

"And now for the lady of the hour. Your honor, it's my great pleasure to introduce to you the artistic director of The Marxist Sisters, Ms. Teena Mildow."

51

The Mayor's interest piqued as the attractive woman dressed all in black stepped toward him, boots clicking, hand confidently extended. He took her hand, quickly drew her close and kissed her firmly on the cheek. "The honor is mine. Ms Mildow. I've been following your career for quite some time. It's artists like you, dedicated to their craft, overcoming insurmountable obstacles to present their work, that help make New York the great city it is." He pulled he close again, kissed her other cheek, then let Teena's hand slide slowly from his. Teena, teetering momentarily on her spike heels, waved her hand and opened her mouth as if to speak, but said nothing as the Mayor's gaze washed over her. Turning to the reporters on the sidewalk, the Mayor continued.

"Ladies and gentlemen of the press, I don't have to tell you how excited and proud I am to be here tonight to announce the Department of Cultural Affairs new grant underwriting production costs for the 2024 season of The Marxist Sisters. Only in the greatest city in the world could a radical lesbian theater company, espousing the destruction of the free market economy and strict segregation of the sexes, receive public money to further their cause. And while some might question the use of public funds to support such an organization, I say to them this is an example of our strength. The City of New York is not afraid of difference – it is this very diversity that will lead us through the 21st century. Black, white, gay, straight, man, woman, capitalist and communist, New York embraces them. Let us sit together at the table of joy. There are crumbs enough for all! So without further ado, it is my great pleasure to pronounce 2024 as the year …"

The squeal of brakes drown out the Mayor's voice. The crowd turned to look as a vehicle that resembled nothing so much as a piece of apple pie topped with a slice of cheddar cheese came to a halt at the curb. As church bells chimed seven, the passenger door opened and out jumped a small black cat with greenish-yellow eyes and a bright red tongue.

"Mer–ee-owll"

Pieface O'Riley knew how to make an entrance.

13

The Pie Wagon always turned heads. It wasn't everyday that you saw an oversize, steaming piece of pie parked on the pavement. The fact that a silky feline sporting a diamond and platinum collar attached to a black leather leash was among the passengers only made things more interesting. And when a shapely ankle above a deep-blue pump followed the feline out the door, people really took notice. Jaq stepped onto the sidewalk, the strapless blue silk sheath dress she wore a perfect match for her eyes, the shiny leash dangling from her wrist. Zach exited the Pie Wagon, carrying a custom-made, temperature-controlled, round anvil case, 12 inches in diameter, the handcuff welded to its side attached to his right wrist. Dressed in a black linen suit and sporting the obligatory Jerry Garcia tie, he carried something resembling a cane in his left hand. Joining Jaq, with Pieface leading the way, the three blithely strolled by the clowder of reporters, the Mayor, Daisy, Constance, Teena, the rest of The Marxist Sisters and a collection of characters from Beaver Street. Mounting the steps leading into the building, they entered the Playhouse. As the crowd filed in around them, Zach handed his cane to Jaq, who, pulling a tube here and releasing a catch there, converted it into a stand. Zach placed the anvil case atop this contraption, which held it in a surprisingly sturdy fashion. He then unlocked the handcuff, flipped the eight catches securing the lid of the case, and gracefully removed the top. The foyer was instantly filled the fragrance of caramelized onions, molasses and pastrami. The brown beans gleamed, steam rose in curls and a flaky crust encompassing this optical and olfactory treat. Jaq produced a white linen napkin, which she draped

54

over Zach's left arm. Slipping the silver top of the anvil case behind his back, Zach looked around at the bright eyes and watering lips of the gathered group.

"Pie," Zach said in a modest voice, "is served."

MAYOR MIKE'S CHILL-PILL BEAN PIE

For the beans
>1 cup northern white beans
>1 tsp salt
>1 whole onion, peeled
>½ lb. pastrami, end cut, chopped
>1/3 cup blackstrap molasses
>1 tbsp dry mustard
>1 tbsp fresh ground black pepper
>12 2mg Xanax, ground

For the topping
>2 tbsp extra virgin olive oil
>2 large Vidalia onions, sliced extra thin
>salt
>2 tbsp Balsamic vinegar
>1½ tsp Turbinando sugar
>1 tbsp blackstrap molasses

For the crust
>1½ cup flour
>1 tsp salt
>½ cup Crisco
>cold water

Rinse beans and soak in 2 cups cold water overnight. Drain well and place in stockpot or large saucepan. Cover with cold water 2 inches above beans. Add salt, bring to boil quickly. Lower heat and simmer 30 minutes, stirring occasionally. Drain. Place whole onion in ovenproof pottery crock. Add beans and pastrami. Combine molasses with spices and Xanax, pour over beans. Fill crock with boiling water to cover beans, cover and place in 250' oven. Cook 3 hours, stirring and adding more hot water as required.

Heat olive oil in a large cast iron skillet. Add onions and salt and cook over high heat, stirring constantly, till onions are golden. Add vinegar and sugar, reduce heat and partially cover skillet. Cook and stir till onions are nicely browned, about 15 minutes.

Combine dry ingredients for crust. Using a pastry comb, cut in lard. Add water as necessary till dough comes together. Separate dough into one large and one small ball. Roll small ball first. Cut rolled dough into 4" strips. Line sides of 9" springform pan with dough, joining strips as necessary. Roll out remaining dough. Place in bottom of pan, pressing lightly to join with edges.

Remove pastrami from beans, chop coarsely. Set aside ¼ of meat for topping. Return chopped meat to bean mixture. Stir, then turn into unbaked crust. Cover beans with caramelized onions, sprinkle with remaining pastrami, drizzle with molasses. Cook in 350 oven 45 minutes, till crust turns golden brown. Cool 15 minutes before releasing pan spring.

Serves 6-10

14

The Mayor made sure the line formed quickly.

"Zach, that looks great and smells even better. Cut me a nice big piece – I'm famished."

"With pleasure, your honor. After all, I made it especially for you." Zach placed a healthy wedge on a plate he pulled from a compartment in the pie case. "Who's next – ladies?"

"Artists first." Daisy declared. "Go on Teena, you've earned it."

Zach dished up another slice. "How about the cast?" he inquired.

"The cast will not be eating at this time." S. Shurtz announced.

"Why not? They look like they've been living on nuts and berries." Jaq had noticed the hollow cheeks and sunken eyes of the actrons.

"Precisely. We go on weekly foraging trips to MacCarren Park," the stage manager replied. "To increase their awareness and improve their timing, the performers are on a strict vegan diet of raw foods."

Zach wrinkled his nose. "Raw food? The oven is the cornerstone of civilization."

"We are revolutionaries. Civilization, as you call it, is slavery. We do not line the pockets of the utility barons by participating in such a bourgeois activity as baking.

"More for the rest of us. Daisy, CC?"

"You better believe I'm having some. I paid a fucking grand for this sucker."
Daisy sashayed over to Zach and took a plate.

"Just a tiny slice for me." said Constance as she tiptoed to the case.

"You eat like a damn bird. I suppose you'd prefer the MacCarren Park special." Daisy said with a mouthful of beans.

"Who's next?"

Teena noticed Shy eyeing the pie hungrily. "Shy, why don't you have some."

"Well, if Comrade Shurtz doesn't mind …"

"You are not a performer, Comrade Koslowski. If you want to poison yourself with this disgusting amalgam of animal flesh and dairy products, be my guest."

"I hate to disappoint you, but I'm not about to mix meat and dairy in a pie I'm making for the mayor." Zach's eyes narrowed as he spoke. "And calling pastrami 'animal flesh' is like calling the Marx Brothers a comedy team."

"I prefer to call a spade a spade," S. Shurtz sniffed as she turned to address the cast. "Comrades, it's time for final preparations. Back to the dressing room."

With a few furtive glances at the pie case, the performers marched single file down the hall. Zach handed a plate to Shy, who quickly took a forkful.

"This is fantastic, Mr. Mack. I can't remember the last time I had real food."

"What's up with Adelle Davis?" Jaq asked as she watched the cast disappear through the dressing room door.

"You mean Comrade Shurtz? She's the stage manager."

"That explains it. A no-talent power freak."

"S. Schurtz is the best stage manager in New York City." Teena broke in.

59

"S. Shurtz?" Zach said with a laugh. "What's the S stand for – Stalin?"

"Your little joke doesn't change things. S. Shurtz is totally dedicated to The Marxist Sisters. The company couldn't exist without her."

"How unfortunate for you," Jaq said with a frown.

"Mer-ee-owll" added Pieface.

"I think I'll have another one of those units." The Mayor was eying the remaining pie. "Then I've got to go. Running the City of New York is a full-time job, you know."

"Oh, you have to stay to see the rehearsal!" said Teena, grabbing the Mayor's lapel and fixing him with her hazel gaze.

Looking at Teena's hazel eyes as he took another bite of pie, the Mayor felt a little lightheaded. "What's wrong with me? I must be out of shape." he thought. "I only had a pint." Teena was going on about The Marxist Sisters. The Mayor didn't hear a word she was saying. "This babe has the most incredible eyes – Maybe I should stick around."

"All right, all right - you've convinced me. Daisy knows how much I love the theater. The congestion pricing plans can wait. Let me call my driver."

"Thank you so much, Mr. Mayor. You won't regret it."

"I'm sure I won't. And call me Mike." The Mayor was polishing off the last of his pie.

"I feel like the Wooly Mammoth at the Natural History Museum – completely stuffed." Daisy pulled Teena off the Mayor's arm. "The show's about to start, right? Let's go sit down."

"Mer-ee-owll" Pieface O'Riley was slinking around Shy's ankles.

"Looks like Pieface found a friend. Won't you join us, miss …?" Jaq gently touched Shy's arm.

"Sioban – Sioban Koslowski. But call me Shy, everyone else does."

"All right, Shy. Let's go find a seat."

"I'm sorry, I can't. I have to go to the dressing room."

"But I thought Nuts'n'Berries said you weren't in the cast." Zach asked.

"Oh, I'm not. I'm the dramaturge."

"The dramaturge? What's that?"

"It's kind of hard to explain. When it's an original play, the dramaturge helps the playwright with the arrangement of the scenes and the movement of the plot. With published plays, the dramaturge compares different versions of the text, then assembles a script that's closest to the author's original intention."

"How many versions of "The Cocoanuts" are there?"

"Well, there's the stage version, and the screenplay."

"Is there a big difference between the two?"

"Not really. I don't know why The Marxist Sisters need a dramaturge, but I don't care. I just want to work in the theater. Listen, I've got to get going. I need to be in place at the start of the runthrough."

"Where is that?"

"I sit in the dressing room. There's an intercom so I can hear what's happening onstage. I follow the text to make sure no one make any mistakes."

"Sounds fascinating."

"Life in the theater isn't all glory. Everyone has to do their job if the revolution is going to be successful. I've got to run. Comrade Schurtz will be upset if I'm late."

"We certainly don't want that. The Comrade is unpleasant enough as it is. Run along, we'll see you afterward."

Shy waved to the Macks as she ran off down the hall.

"What a sweet kid. How'd she end up with these crackpots?" Jaq wondered to Zach as they entered the performance space.

"Following the siren song of the theater."

"Mer-ee-owll"

"You tell him, Pieface. I don't know why, but I'm worried about her."

"You should have had another piece of pie."

15

Zach Mack had called it right – everyone did love the performance. The Mayor, sitting between Daisy and Teena, laughed so hard he almost fell off his chair. Teena didn't take a single note, she was so pleased with the Mayor's response. Daisy belched and beamed. She didn't even yell at Constance, who had a hard time following the story but liked the part where Groucho, Chico and Harpo entered sporting strap-on dildos. "I guess that means they're men." she decided. Zach couldn't believe his eyes when the cast suddenly began doing jumping jacks, and Jaq enjoyed the music. S. Schurtz was in her glory, seated at the production table with a metronome and a stopwatch, waving a baton as the cast made their entrances and exits, banging on the big drum to mark the end of each scene. Only Shy felt disappointed. Sitting in the darkened dressing room, following the script with a penlight, she couldn't shake the sense that something was wrong. "I thought it would be different," she thought to herself. "If this is the revolution, why am I so sleepy?"

16

Shy awoke with a start. The room was dark except for her penlight, which threw a narrow beam along the floor where it lay. Someone had a handful of her short red hair and was pulling hard. She could feel a sharp object being pressed into her neck, just below her ear.

"You fell asleep," a voice hissed. "Do you know what Lenin did to sentries who fell asleep on duty?"

17

The atmosphere in the performance space was so festive it almost penetrated the gloom of the black box. Teena was being lavished with praise by the Mayor and Daisy, while Zach and Jaq complimented the cast. The performing company of The Marxist Sisters gave new meaning to the expression 'a motley crew'. There was Teri Haari from Helsinki, who looked like a birch sapling in an Yvonne De Carlo wig. She had played Groucho. Zach asked her what it was like to portray an American comedy icon, but Teri just shrugged. It turned out she spoke no English and had learned her lines phonetically. Papa Kupe, The Sisters' Chico, was Maori – all 340 pounds of her. "That explains the tattoos." Jaq smiled after kissing Papa on the cheek. "I thought they were meant to be an indictment of the enslavement of the working class."

"No, that's why I wore blackface." It was Keisha Zamira, a diminutive African-American who had portrayed Harpo.

"I was wondering about that. I thought blackface was off-limits because of its racist and imperialist implications." Zach towered over Keisha as he spoke.

"Of course, you're right. But the revolutionary uses any tools at their disposal. By embracing this image of oppression and making the personal choice to embody it, I empower myself by inverting a symbol of domination and creating one of liberation."

"If you say so. Anyway, I loved your performance. I'm a big Marx Brothers fan." Zach shook Keisha's hand as he spoke.

"The cult of personality that surrounds those lackeys is of no significance." Keisha snapped.

"Well, in that case, we hated these lackeys you portrayed so charmingly. Zach, I think we should be going. Pieface is getting antsy." Jaq was searching in her purse for the leash.

"Let's say goodbye to Daisy."

18

Mayor Mike was reaching for his Blackberry.

"Don't call your driver yet," cried Teena, taking a firm grip on the Mayor's hand. "I want to show you the rest of our facility."

"I don't know, I've got a meeting about rescinding term limits first thing tomorrow."

"I'll give you the whirlwind tour. See you at home later, Daisy!" Teena blew a quick kiss, then took the Mayor by the arm and led him down the hall.

"What's got her all wet between the knees? If I didn't know her better, I'd swear she's trying to get into his pants." Daisy fussed as she walked out of the theater.

"Well, you know how much Ms. Mildow enjoys wearing slacks." Constance offered. "Shall I call the limo?"

"There you are." Zach's voice boomed down the hall. "I couldn't leave without thanking you for the business."

"I'll give you the business, all right, and your lovely wife, too. Just keep that damn cat away from me."

"Mer-ee-oowl"

"Pieface doesn't like it when you swear at him." Jaq tugged gently at his leash.

"Jesus Christ, you think I give a flying fuck what a cat thinks? Listen, my limo is on the way. Can I drop you kids somewhere?"

"No, we've got the Pie Wagon."

"OK, then, till tomorrow. And don't burn the damn custard!"

"Not burned – scorched. Just the way you like it."

"Very funny, Pieman. Stick to your fuckin' oven and leave the comedy to the professionals. I gotta get back to Manhattan – where is CC? I can only take so fucking much of fucking Bushwick. Goddam it, where the fuck are you?" Daisy went screaming down the hall.

"And a lovely evening to you as well." Zach offered to the receding yellow mound. "Let's make our move, my dear."

"OK. C'mon, Pieface."

"Mer-ee-owll"

"You can't like it here that much .."

"Mer-ee-OWLL"

"I heard you, now let's .."

"MER-ee-OWLL"

"Pieface, what is the matter with you?" Jaq knelt down to pet the cat, when with a start, Pieface suddenly took off running down the hall, pulling the leash out of Jaq's hand. In a flash all you could see was a twinkling snake of diamonds and platinum slipping around the corner.

19

They had barely turned the corner when Teena spun, and without letting go of the Mayor's arm, grabbed his dick as well. Even Mayor Mike was surprised at his instantaneous response.

"Like I said, I want to show you the rest of our facility." Teena bit Mayor Mike's ear. "Here's something really impressive." Slipping her hand from the Mayor's arm, Teena reached back and opened the door behind her, pulling them into an empty broom closet. Loosening his belt and unzipping his fly, she dropped the Mayor's pants to his ankles. "Boxers – how cute." With a tug, off they came. "I understand you are the Mayor of the City of New York." Teena addressed his rigidness with a flick of her forefinger. Then, turning as she slipped her jeans over her hips, she said, "Would you mind proving it?"

"I guess it's time to embrace radical feminist lesbianism." the Mayor determined.

20

Pieface was scratching at the theater door when the Macks caught up with him.

"Mer-ee-owll … mer-ee-oe-owll … mer-ii-ee-io-e-owll"

"What's got him going? I've never seen him like this." Jaq grabbed the end of the leash that was flipping over the floor. She tried the knob. "The door's locked!"

"Not for long." Zach took a breath, then charged a few steps, lowering his shoulder. The door popped open easily. "Ladies first." he said, straightening his tie.

The theater was dark except for the ghost light. Tied to the pole was a figure resembling St. Sebastian, with No. 2 pencils in place of arrows. Stepping closer, Zach and Jaq could make out the grey pants, a t-shirt, then a shock of red hair.

"It's Shy!" Jaq cried as she ran toward the girl. She turned Shy's shoulder and saw the yellow shaft of a No. 2 pencil, its pink eraser like a rosebud, rising out of a dark blotch on the girl's left breast. "Zach, call 911!"

"I'm on it. Where's Pieface?"

"Mer-ee-owll"

Out of the blackness, a woman's voice shrieked.

"Holy Mother of God, get this damn cat off of me!" S. Shurtz slipped from the shadows, falling onto her back. Firmly clamped onto her breasts was Pieface O'Riley.

"Pieface doesn't like it when you swear at him. And what would Chairman Mao think – Holy Mother of God? "

"I don't care, I'm sorry, just make him stop – he's killing me!"

"From the looks of things, it's a taste of your own medicine." Zach stepped over S. Shurtz supine body. "Good work, Pieface. You keep her covered. The cops are on their way. How's Shy?"

"She's alive, at least. But her breathing is shaky and her pulse is racing.

"Get something wrapped around that pencil and keep pressure on her chest."

"Give me your tie."

"My tie? Are you kidding? This is a Collection One!"

"I'll use it to wring your neck if you don't give to me. Now hurry – this girl needs help!"

Zach looked at Shy's pale face beneath her red hair, then quickly undid his tie. He was handing it to Zach when the police and EMT crew burst through the door.

"Saved by the bell. Over here, boys, we've got a bleeder."

"Take care of that one. Everybody else, just stay where you are." The police sergeant's voice rang in the empty theater like a church bell. "Who called 911!"

"That would be me, officer." Zach took a step forward.

"I said stay where you are. This is a murder investigation."

"Murder? No, she's still alive!" Jaq cried out.

"That one, maybe. But not the one out front."

"Out front?"

"Yeah, lying on the front steps of the building. Female, Caucasian, maybe early 30's, medium height, trim build, eye color undetermined. Dressed in a black t-shirt, black jeans."

71

"That sounds like Comrade Mildow." S. Shurtz grunted. "But what did you mean, eye color undetermined? Her eyes are the most beautiful shade of hazel."

The Macks looked at Shurtz with surprise. So did the sergeant. "Hey, lady, you know you got a cat stuck to your tits?"

"Yes officer, I know I've got a cat stuck to my tits. Now what about the eyes?"

"Oh, yeah, well, they may have been a beautiful shade of hazel, but not any more."

"What do you mean?" Zach asked.

"Looks like somebody went at them with a bootheel or something. There's nothin' left but two bloody holes."

21

Locust Street was a blaze of flashing red lights. Police cruisers, ambulances, unmarkeds with rotating cherries on their dashboards, even a hook and ladder at the end of the block. A helicopter hovered overhead, its harsh spotlight trained on the front entrance of The Courtyard Playhouse. The body of Teena Mildow lay sprawled on the steps, head on the sidewalk, face up. An occasional red light would cut through the fierce white glare from the helicopter, catching glistening blood on the forehead and cheeks. Yellow crime scene tape boxed off the sidewalk. Radios squealed as the sirens of newly arriving police vehicles wailed. Teena Mildow would have been impressed – it was a very dramatic setting.

Doors opened and several extremely large men in black and gray suits got out of cars which had just pulled up. They stood at the curb looking at the body on the sidewalk. From a sleek silver Toyota parked in the middle of the street, two even larger uniformed cops hopped out. Behind them, at the bottom of a pair of legs which could barely be glimpsed, spots of red danced across two of the shiniest black shoes ever polished.

"Let me see her."

The two groups of large men parted and the Commissioner of Police of the City of New York walked up to the crime scene. William Raymond III was a man of equal proportions. He was 4'6" tall and wore a 54" jacket over 54" waist trousers. His shoe size was 8, same as his hat, although he never wore one. William Raymond III was enough of a politician to know better than to hide his star under a bushel. So he never wore a hat. Instead, he displayed his trademark attribute – a full head of curly white hair. He looked like a Chia Pet on a milk diet.

Nimbly slipping under the yellow tape, the Commissioner approached the body of Tina Mildow. The empty stare was unsettling, even to William Raymond III, fourth-generation NYPD. He spoke to the large suits.

"Get that helicopter out of here – it's making too much racket. What's up with the hook and ladder? I don't smell fire. Why do we need three ambulances? Move 'em. Get these people off the street – show's over, time to go home. Reporters? Send 'em back to the bar. No comment now – press conference later. Cover that body – it gives me the creeps. And where's the other boot?"

22

Parked in the private garage of the townhouse at 1 E 69 Street, a phone rang in the back seat of the Suburban. Without sitting up, Mayor Michael Hindenberg answered.

"Who's calling me on this number? Oh, hello, Bill. Little late for a chat, pal. Did you pull over some drunken Staten Island Congressman or something? Yes, I was in Bushwick tonight. That's right, The Courtyard Playhouse. No, I ended up staying. I had the time of my life, why? I don't know, maybe an hour ago – what time is it anyway? What's with all the questions –Oh.

Oh.

Oh.

No.

That's why you're the Commissioner, Billy Boy. Don't call again– Mikey needs his beauty rest."

The Mayor reached for the door latch, opened it and threw the phone onto the garage floor. Leaving the door ajar, he rolled over and went back to sleep.

23

"How's she doing? Will she be all right?" Jaq was hovering over the EMT worker bandaging Sky's punctures.

"She's in pretty good shape, all in all. I was able to close all the wounds. She's lucky those pencils were so sharp. There's a possibility of graphite poisoning, but the bleeding actually helps there – cleans things out."

"How fortunate." Zach mumbled, looking a little unsteady.

"Zach has trouble with blood – he faints when he sees it." Jaq laughed.

"Why don't you sit down, sir." The sergeant's voice tolled. "I'll put a set of cuffs on this one, if we can just …"

"Sally? What are you doing here? And why is there a cat stuck to your tits?"

"It's a long story, Emily."

"Sally … Emily … " the sergeant looked from the EMT worker to the stage manager. "You two know each other?"

"Know each other – that's my sister, Sally Shurtz."

"Sally?" Zach looked quizzically at the feline-fronted radical.

"No wonder she billed herself as 'S. Shurtz'." Jaq giggled. "Who ever heard of a revolutionary named Sally?"

"Oh, Sally, are you still trying to smash the state? You know how much that upsets Mom and Dad."

"I have no parents but the party."

"I saw Freddy last week – he asked about you. I told him I hadn't seen you in years. You should give him a call – he's such a sweetheart."

"I have no time for men. I live for the revolution."

"You won't have to worry about no men, lady." The sergeant's voice rang out. "Not where they'll be sending you. Now, will someone get this damn cat off this lady's boobs?"

"Pieface doesn't like it when you swear at him." Jaq admonished the officer. Then, kneeling "Good kitty, let go, that's right, get those claws out, now don't scratch, we've got this one covered."

"Mer-ee-owl" Pieface O'Riley made a quick leap to the floor, then trotted over to Shy and began licking her chin.

"I told you he liked you – how are you feeling?"

Shy tried to answer, but Emily cut in.

"Now you just lay there, young lady. No talking, no moving. We're going to get you into an ambulance in a minute and get you over to Woodhull. It's right down the block."

The sergeant's radio squwaked. "Sergeant Muldoon, do you read, over."

"Copy, base, Muldoon here."

"Commissioner is out in front the building. He wants to talk to the officer who found the body."

"That would be me, base. Copy. Will report to the Commissioner stat."

"Body … commissioner … is this all because of me?" Shy had a look of panic on her face.

77

"No, honey, but there's some bad news. Teena Mildow is dead – murdered right outside the building."

"Oh, no, Teena …."

"She had it coming." S. Shurtz said contemptuously. "The way she subjugated herself to the Mayor tonight. The Mayor – a capitalist pig if there ever was one. And a man on top of that."

"That's the kind of talk that got you into this trouble, Sally." Emily was wagging her finger at her sister. "The Mayor is a wonderful man."

"Oh, shut up, Emily"

"Why don't you both shut up," the sergeant's voice pealed. "McShea, get over here and keep an eye on this one. And don't let anyone leave this room."

"Yes, sir, Sergeant." The rookie saluted the sergeant's back.

"Mer-ee-owll" In a flash, Pieface zipped through the door.

"Oh, Pieface, no!" Jaq called out, following the small black cat.

"Excuse, me, miss, but the sergeant said …"

"Yes, we heard the sergeant, but the cat's out of the bag, so to speak." Zach interrupted. "He told you to keep an eye on the prisoner."

"Yes, sir, but he also said …"

"We won't go far. Don't abandon your post, officer." Zach said as he stepped through the damaged doorway.

"All right, now. That's it. Nobody else is going anywhere." Officer McShea said with all the authority he could muster.

"We're not going anywhere, officer. I haven't had a chance to talk to my sister in years." Emily chimed in. "So, tell me, Sally, do you still do needlepoint?"

S. Shurtz groaned the groan of the oppressed workers of the world.

24

"She claims to have seen the whole thing, Commissioner." One of the large uniforms was talking.

"The Mayor, too?

"Yes, sir, the Mayor, too."

"Bring her over, then."

William Raymond III was standing in the middle of Locust Street smoking a cigar. Things had quieted down. The helicopter no longer thwacked the night sky, only a few police cars and one ambulance remained on the block. A white cloth covered Teena Mildow's body like napkin over a rack of ribs at a greasy bar-b-que joint. The yellow tape snapped in the fitful breeze. The large uniform returned with a moon-faced black woman not much more than skin and bones. Her brownish hair was pulled up around the temples, where it lay scraggily on the top of her head. She wore a faded blouse of fuchsia satin which might have been pretty at one time. Now, stained with water, wine and who knows what else, threadbare with fraying lace around the neckline, it just looked sad. Wobbling across the street, the woman's gaze slid from side to side with a woozy rhythm, following a tennis match only she could see. The uniform gestured toward the Commissioner.

"Tell this gentleman what you saw."

After a few attempts, the woman's eyes settled on the Commissioner's face.

"Ooh, what pretty hair! Can I touch it? Ooh, it tickles. What's your name, Fuzzy? I'm Fuchsia."

"Excuse me, miss, please take your fingers off the commissioner's hair. This is William Raymond III, Commission ..."

"Hey, Fuzzy, tell Coppertop to put a lid on it. You got a cigarette?"

"It's all right, officer. Go find me a cigarette for the young lady."

"Hah – that's rich! I ain't young and I sure as hell ain't no lady. But that don't matter, Fuzzy, I know a few tricks them little girlies never learnt. Forget the cigarette, gimme one of them big things you're burnin'."

Commissioner Raymond pulled a cigar case from his jacket pocket. Fuchsia grabbed it and took the two panatelas it held. "Ooh, these smell good! Fuchsia says thank you very much. Now gimme a light."

The Commissioner flinched slightly as the end of one his hand-rolled Cuban-seed Dominican cigars went up in flame. "Pretty!" Fuchsia exclaimed. "Ouch! Burnt my fingers." She picked the stogie off the sidewalk and took a big puff. "Watch me blow a smoke ring."

"I'd much rather hear about what you saw earlier."

"You mean with Black Lady and Big Yellow?"

"I'm mean when you saw the Mayor."

"Oh, sure, the Cheez Whiz." A cloud of cigar smoke clung to the split ends of Fuchsia's hair. "Not much with him. He come out the door with Black Lady."

"There was a black woman with the Mayor?"

"There weren't no black woman – it was Black Lady. You know, the one lyin' on the steps, killt, eyes poked out. Anyway, she's all over him. Actin' like me

81

when I got to score bad. He tryin' kinda keep her at bay, ya know? Like when you holding a cat what fell into a gallon a paint. Then the Hummer pull up."

"There was a HumVee?"

"I don't know – the ride like Jay-Z you know, big, black, smooth –"

"The Mayor's Suburban."

"'F you say so. So Cheez Whiz open a door on a Hummer, be climbin' in, when Black Lady grabs his ass."

"The victim grabbed the Mayor's buttocks?"

"She din't look like no victim to me – she was doin' the victimatin'. What I meant was she grabbed Cheezy's pants or belt or sumthin', pulled him back to the sidewalk, then kisses him like she want his teeth to come out."

"The victim kissed the Mayor."

"I already tol' you who were bein' victimated. Well, while this be happenin', Big Yellow come out the buildin'."

"Big Yellow? Who's that?"

"I don' know 'f it was a who, but it was plenty big and sure 'nough yellow. So, Big Yellow just standin' there, face turnin' kinda red. When the Whiz sees her, he waves his hand says something – Hello, Dolly, I think. Then Black Lady head spin so fast I thought her neck gonna snap. She turn to Big Yellow, take a step. Well, the Mayor, then, he jump inna back a the Hummer, and off they go, screetchin' tires and all like teevee."

"And that was it?"

"No, they plenty more."

82

"I mean with the Mayor. When he left, the victim was still alive."

"You mean Black Lady? Yeah, she standin' there, all right."

"And the Mayor had left."

"Geez, how dumb is you? Nuthin' worse than a stupid cop. The Mayor been gone and Black Lady be standin' there watch smoke come out a Big Yellow's ears. That's when Mouse showed up."

"A mouse appeared?"

"Damn, Fuzz, this a nice smoke. Kinda strong, though."

"You're not supposed to inhale."

"Hah – not inhale. That's like drinkin' without swallowin'. Who you think I am, Big Bubba? Me and my man Barack, we inhale!"

"Tell me more about this mouse. Where did it come from, the garbage can? Did it bite someone?"

"Oh, Fuzzy, you funny. I think you been a cop too long. No, there weren't no bitin'. Big Yellow spittin' mad – I mean for real. She give Black Lady a faceful. Well, Black Lady go at her, scratching at her eyes, when Mouse …"

"What did the mouse do?"

"Sorry, Fuz, feelin' kinda funny. Let me hold onna your arm. Like I said, Black Lady be scratching, and then …"

"Then what? What happened with the mouse?"

'What happened was this … Oh, Fuzzy …" And clutching the sleeve of William Raymond III vicuna overcoat, Fuschia leaned forward and puked all over two of the shiniest black shoes ever polished.

83

25

Sergeant Muldoon stepped out of the Courtyard Playhouse just as Fuchsia was spoiling the Commissioner's shoeshine.

"Sergeant Muldoon, Commissioner. What can I do for you?" he said with a salute.

"Right now, Sergeant," William Raymond III said as he took his cigar from his mouth, "You can detach this witness from my sleeve and have someone give her medical attention. Then tell my driver to get my extra pair of shoes from the trunk."

The sergeant pulled Fuchsia free and handed her to one of the large uniforms standing awkwardly beside the Commissioner, then dispatched a large suit in search of the driver.

"I was first on the scene, sir," said the sergeant, saluting again. "I found the body."

"You found the body?"

"Yes, sir."

"Anything else?"

"Sir?"

"Did you find anything else?"

"No, sir. I radioed for another unit, then entered the building."

"You entered the building?"

"Yes, sir. I was responding to a 911 call. There was an attempted murder in progress."

84

"An attempted murder in progress?"

"Yes, sir. Apparently, the stage manager went berserk and attacked the dramaturge with a handful of No. 2 pencils."

"No. 2 pencils?"

"Yes, sir."

The Commissioner's driver arrived with the extra shoes and a small camp stool. William Raymond III sat as the driver changed his shoes for him.

"The dramaturge, you say?"

"Yes, sir."

"Just what is a dramaturge, Sergeant?"

"I have no idea, Commissioner. I'm not even sure what a stage manager is, sir."

"What does any of that have to do with this?" William Raymond III asked, gesturing to the body of Teena Mildow.

"I couldn't tell you, Commissioner."

"Well, we need to find some someone who can."

"Mer-ee-owl"

A black streak shot through the front door of the Courtyard Playhouse and out onto Locust Street. William Raymond III leapt to his feet. Several of the large uniforms began chasing it when it suddenly leapt onto the white shroud covering the body of Teena Mildow.

"Come here, you damn cat!" one of them hollered.

"Pieface doesn't like it when you swear at him."

85

The uniforms looked up with a start at Jaq Mack, standing resplendent at the top of the steps in her blue silk dress and patent leather pumps, swinging the diamond and platinum leash. Zach Mack, his black linen suit barely wrinkled, stood beside her smoothing his tie.

"Having trouble, officer? Perhaps we can be of assistance."

26

Zach strode down the steps to the sidewalk of Locust Street. "Allow me to introduce myself, Commissioner Raymond. Zach Mack, Piemaker to the Stars. This is my wife Jaq."

"Pleased to meet you. Nice tie. And I suppose that would be the famous Pieface O'Riley confounding my security detail." The Commissioner cast a bemused look at the group of uniforms surrounding the body of Teena Mildow. "New York's finest."

"Don't blame your men." Jaq purred. "Pieface can be a handful." Shaking the diamond and platinum collar, Jaq clicked her tongue a few times. Pieface darted between a couple of the large uniforms and jumped into Jaq's arms. "You just have to know how to talk to him."

"What happened out here, Commissioner?"

"I was just about to ask you that question, Mr. Mack."

"No idea. We were busy inside. It was the Sergeant who informed us about the murder."

"You called 911?"

"I did."

Having attached Pieface to his leash, Jaq set the cat down on the sidewalk. "A member of the company was being attacked." she said, "We didn't know anything about what was happening to poor Teena."

"Yes, I heard the stage manager stabbed the drama... dramaterm... drama-tang..." William Raymond III searched for the word.

"Dramaturge," said Zach, coming to the Commissioner's rescue. "Turned her into a pin cushion, except she used No. 2 pencils."

"No. 2 pencils. Yes. So, you didn't know anything about what was happening to poor Teena."

"Didn't I just say that?" Jaq gave the Commissioner an exasperated look. "Teena had gone off with the Mayor, and we were saying goodnight to Daisy Mac-Dailey ..."

"Daisy MacDailey was here?"

"How else could we have spoken to her?" Jaq replied sharply. "She was with CC ..."

"CC?"

"Constance Carruthers, Ms. MacDailey's assistant." Zach answered. "They were waiting for their limo."

"They were waiting for their limo."

"Excuse me, Commissioner." It was one of the large uniforms. "We've completed our search of the area. No sign of anyone or anything unusual."

"No boot?" William Raymond III addressed the officer.

"Sir?"

"The victim was missing one boot. No sign of it?"

"No, sir, no sign of a boot."

"Thank you, officer. Now, Mr. Mack, where were we?"

"Daisy MacDailey and Constance Carruthers were waiting for their limo."

"Yes. That's right. They were waiting for their limo."

"Pieface wants to go for a walk. I'll leave the Pete and RePete act to you two." Jaq let the small black cat with greenish-yellow eyes and a bright red tongue lead her down the block.

"You'll excuse my wife, Commissioner. She tires easily."

"She tires easily?"

"Exactly."

"Well, Mr. Mack, neither you nor your wife have been of much help here. I'm still left with a corpse and plenty of questions. So, unless you have something additional to offer, I'm going to have to ask you to leave the crime scene to the professionals."

"Nothing would give me greater pleasure, Commissioner Raymond. I'll just collect my wife and cat …"

"Mer-ee-owll"

Pieface O'Riley had jumped atop a metal garbage can and was scratching at it furiously.

"Ooh, I think he's found a mouse!" Jaq shrieked. "Zac, come get him. You know how much I hate mice. Hurry!"

"I'll be right there, dear. The Commissioner was just giving us the brush."

"Mer-ee-OWLL" Pieface clawed the metal cover.

"Cat on a hot tin garbage can. Come on, boy, time to go home."

"MER-ee-OWLL" As Zach lifted Pieface, the cat grabbed the lid handle with his paws. "Mer-EE-owll" Pieface pulled the lid off the can.

"Oh, my God, Zach ..." Jaq gasped.

"Didn't expect to find you here. What's with the Ali Baba routine?"

"Mer-ee-owl"

Hunched in the can amid the garbage, covering her face with her daily calendar, was Constance Carruthers.

27

"Hey, it's Mouse! You foun' her. She the one!" Fuchsia's cackled over the crackle of police radios. She was hanging out the rear door of an ambulance. "Fuzzy! It's her - Mouse!"

William Raymond III looked up from the garbage can. "She's Mouse?"

"Damn, Fuzz, you is the dummest cop ever lived. Whad I jus' say? She the one – Mouse. She did it."

"She did it."

"I'm gonna smack you up the side of your head you do that one more time. I'm tellin' ya – she killt Black Lady. After Black Lady hit Big Yellow."

"Big Yellow?" Zach asked, looking at Fuchsia.

"Don't you start in now. Fuzzy know who I'm talking about. Black Lady and Big Yellow screamin' and cussin', then Black Lady be scratchin' an' slappin' Big Yellow. Mouse show up, start hollerin' at Black Lady, then whack her with this book she be carryin'. Black Lady fall down the steps, crack her skull onna sidewalk. You could hear it clear cross the street. Black Lady jus' layin there. I knew she be dead."

"You knew she be dead."

"Now, what I say, Fuzz? So then, this limo pull up. Mouse push Big Yellow inna back, say get goin', don' worry 'bout me. Limo pull off. That's when I go hide."

William Raymond III turned to Constance Carruthers, who was still cowering in the garbage can. "You have gotten yourself into a very bad spot, Miss. Would you mind stepping out of the can, please?"

Constance struggled getting free from the battered metal trash bin, then stood on the pavement with as much dignity as she could manage.

"What do you have to say to this young lady's accusations?" Fuchia snorted out a laugh as the Commissioner spoke.

"I have nothing to say."

"In that case, you are under arrest. The sergeant will take you to the station house for processing, then you'll be sent to Central Booking. Cuff the suspect, please."

Sergeant Muldoon stepped up to Constance. "Arms behind your back, please."

"Just a minute, Sergeant." The Commissioner interrupted. "Let me see her hands." William Raymond III examined Constance Carruthers immaculate manicure. "OK, she's all yours."

The sergeant slipped the cuffs on the suspect before depositing CC in the back seat of a patrol car. As they were pulling away, Zach spoke to the Commissioner.

"What's with the nail inspection? Making sure she's clean enough for jail?"

"No, Mr. Mack, I was checking to see if there was evidence that she had clawed the victim's eyes."

"Find anything?"

"Nothing whatsoever."

92

"Mer-ee-owl"

"Excuse me, Commissioner, but Pieface has a question for you."

"Go ahead, Mrs. Mack."

"That woman – the one who witnessed the murder …"

"Yes, what about her."

"Pieface wants to know why she's wearing one tennis shoe and one black leather boot."

28

Donny Paloma had spent his life in the Emergency Room of Woodhull Medical Center. His mother had arrived there by taxi twenty minutes before Donny arrived in this world. As a child, he had been treated been in the ER for a broken nose, rheumatic fever and an allergic reaction to a bee sting. Donny was volunteering at the hospital by the time he was 14 and on the payroll at 18. He pulled the lobster shift while getting his Master's Degree in Nursing at Hunter College. Now 28, Donny worked nights as the head nurse in charge of admittance. Donny Paloma had seen a lot at Woodhull – husbands stuck with butcher knives by jealous wives, wives strangled by jealous husbands, babies crushed by their sleeping 300-pound fathers, 15-year old heroin dealers with 16 bullet wounds. Donny had even seen a performance artist who had his wrists slashed while being beaten with florescent tubes by a dominatrix at a gallery in Williamsburg. But when the EMT's rolled Sioban Koslowski in on a gurney and told Donny she had been stabbed with six No. 2 pencils, he was flabbergasted. "Six No. 2 pencils?" he thought. "This town has gone to the dogs."

"That's a very good question your cat has posed, Ms. Mack." William Raymond III ran a hand through his curly locks. "Just why are you wearing one tennis shoe and one black boot, Ms. ...?"

"It's Fuchsia, Fuzzy. I ain't no Mzz nuthin'. And so what if I'm wearin' two diffint shoes. It's the style, you know."

"It's the style?"

"Sure. I read it in the New York Times."

"You read it in the New York Times?"

"Don't start repeatin' y'self again. You heard what I said. What, you don't think I'm smart enough to read the newspaper?"

"I'm certain many people less intelligent than you read the New York Times every day. That boot on your right foot, however, does look like a match with the one on the victim's left foot."

"They's very popular right now."

"She's right, actually," Jaq broke in. "I've been thinking about buying a pair myself."

"All this talk about cobblery is fascinating, Commissioner." It was Zach's turn to interrupt. "But I'm more interested in the eyes. If CC didn't scratch them out, what happened to Teena Mildow's eyes?"

"What happened to Teena Mildow's eyes?"

"Christ, Fuzzy, if you promise to stop with the parrot routine, I'll tell you."

"All right, Fuchsia, tell me. What happened to Teena Mildow's eyes?"

"I et 'em"

"You et them?"

"Dammit, Fuzz, you promised. That's right, I et 'em. Popped 'em out wif my spoon."

"Popped them out with your spoon?"

"That better be the last time, Fuzzy. Yeah, I used my spoon." Pulling at her hair, Fuchsia produced a small spoon with a silver handle and an iridescent bowl.

"Good grief, it's a caviar spoon!" Zach sputtered.

"Got that right, Doughboy. Always keep it handy just in case. You ever et an eyeball? They good – like fish eggs. What you call it – cadaviar? But you got to get 'em quick. Half'n hour after the person dead, they get tough – chewy, you know. Don't like chewy stuff."

"So you ate Ms. Mildow's eyes?"

"Only one of 'em, actually. First one slipt out my hand. They kinda slimy, you know. Went bouncin' down the street. I'm not fussy, but I don't eat nuthin' off the streets in this neighborhood – too dirty."

"I'm afraid I'm going to have to ask you to come downtown, Miss … Fuch-sia."

"Hell, don't be afraid. I been downtown plenty. I like it there – I c'n sleep. Can I ride wif you?" Fuchsia took hold of the Commissioner's lapel and batted her eyelashes.

"I don't think that would be proper procedure. I'll see you after you've been processed."

"Been processed – sounds right, They gonna process me, then put me inna can. Like catfood. Well, see you in a bit." Fuchsia giggled as an officer handcuffed her and led her to a police cruiser. "Oh, officer, handcuffs, my favorite!"

"Just get in the vehicle, ma'am."

William Raymond III watched as Fuchsia tried to wave goodbye, then turned to the Macks. "You've been of great service to the City of New York tonight, Mr. and Ms. Mack. You and your cat as well."

"Mer-ee-owl"

"You'll have to excuse me now. The Department will be in touch if we need a statement."

"We're always ready to do our civic duty, Commissioner," Zach replied, giving William Raymond III's hand a hearty shake.

"Yes, anything we can do, don't hesitate to call." Jaq smiled as the Commissioner bowed slightly.

"Perhaps you could donate something to the Department's next bake sale. Supports the Patrolmen's Benevolent Association."

"Sounds like fun - I'm all for benevolence." Zach said with a grin. "I'll see what I can whip up."

His driver opened the rear door of the sleek silver Toyota and William Raymond III slipped inside. The Macks watched the wavy white orb that was the Commissioner's head disappeared behind the tinted window glass.

"I think Fuchsia might be right." Zach spoke as the Toyota turned right on Broadway.

"What's that, dear?"

"William Raymond III just might be the dumbest cop that ever lived."

"Mer-ee-OWL"

"Come on, Zach. I want to see how Shy is doing. The hospital is right down the block. And you should give Daisy a call."

"Daisy? At this hour?"

"She should get a heads-up on CC. Let's go, Pieface."

30

"How did you get Pieface in here?"

Sioban Koslowski was propped up in her hospital bed, sprouting bandages, as the small black cat with greenish-yellow eyes and a bright red tongue chewed on her ear.

"It wasn't easy. I thought Jaq was going to strangle the nurse with the leash."

"Donny? But he's so nice."

"Not if you walk into his ER accompanied by a cat."

"Yes, felons are welcome at Woodhull, but not felines."

"Now, Jaq. Anyway, we convinced him that Pieface was a certified emotional support animal. But I think it was because we were visiting you. Donny seems to have a soft spot for dramaturges."

"Oh, Mr. Mack, don't tease me. He was awfully sweet, though. It was something about the pencil wounds, I think. But tell me about Teena. What happened to her?"

Jaq filled Shy in about the fight in front of the Courtyard Playhouse, how Teena had fallen and cracked her skull, that it was Daisy MacDailey's assistant who had done it.

"How terrible! Then what, did she scratch her eyes out?"

"Not exactly." Zach didn't think Shy needed all the gory details right now. "It's quite a band of nutcases you got yourself mixed up with."

"I suppose you're right, Mr. Mack. I wasn't paying much attention – I was just so excited to be working in theater."

"What will you do now?"

"I don't know. Maybe I'll move back to Rochester. They say suicide is redundant there, but that may be better than death by No. 2 pencil."

"Mer-ee-owl"

"I agree with Pieface." Jaq was watching as the cat played with Shy's IV. "You've had your baptism into the world of show biz. Hang in there. One thing about New York – you've got to be tough."

"Mer-EE-owl"

"OK, Pieface, I'll sleep on it." Shy laid back with a deep sigh. "This bed is so comfortable. I forgot what a real mattress feels like. I think I could sleep for a week."

"Go right ahead, kiddo. Jaq and I will just slip out the door. You'll hear from us soon."

"Thanks again, Mr. and Mrs. Mack. And you too, Pieface.

"Mer-ee-owl"

The Macks left the Emergency Room of Woodhull Medical Center and headed back to Locust Street, where the Pie Wagon was parked. The police and emergency vehicles had left, the yellow tape marking the crime scene was gone and the body of Teena Mildow removed. Jaq let Pieface off the leash and he went chasing shadows on the sidewalk.

"I'm cold, Zach, could I have your jacket?"

100

"Of course, here you are. Now let's get in the Wagon and get out of here."

Jaq looked around the deserted block. "This street is so lonely. Why would anybody try to put a theater here?"

"Because there's no place else left. There's no room for art in New York anymore."

"So sad. Such a terrible place to die."

"I don't know that there are any good places to die."

"There are plenty of places better than this, that's for sure. I'm glad you didn't tell Shy everything."

"You mean ..."

"You know what I mean. What a crazy story. Do you think it's true?"

"Well, I suppose stranger things have happened, although I can't think of any off hand. Where's Pieface? I want to get out of here."

"Mer-ee-owl"

"There he is, by the curb. What have you got, buddy?"

"Mer-ee-owl"

"What in the world is he fussing with?"

The Macks stepped over to the sidewalk where Pieface was clawing with his prize. Jaq stepped over to pick him up.

"What is it? What are you playing with? Oh my God, Zach ... '

There in the gutter, staring up at Jaq Mack, was a beautiful hazel eyeball that had once belonged to Teena Mildow.

31

"Oyez, oyez. This session of night court is called to order. The Honorable Ruth Lester presiding. You may be seated."

Judge Lester took her seat behind the tribunal. Ruth Lester had been working the night court in lower Manhattan since the Koch administration. The City of New York had been through many changes during her 45-year tenure, but not Judge Lester. With her heavy, oversize glasses dangling from her neck on a jeweled chain, her pageboy haircut, and her Mary Janes, Ruth Lester would have been the epitome of stylish taste as she walked down Maiden Lane in 1979. Tonight, however, she looked like a something in the display case at Yonah Shimmel's – a musty relic from a misty past.

"The case of the State of New York versus Constance Carruthers. The defendant is accused of murder in the second degree of Teena Anne Mildow."

The bailiff led Constance into the courtroom. In the orange prison jumpsuit, she looked very slight. Constance's hands searched for her calendar like an amputee with ghost limb syndrome.

Judge Lester balanced her glasses on the bridge of her nose as she reviewed the court papers. "Ms. Carruthers, you stand before me accused of a very serious crime. Do you have a lawyer to represent you? If not, the court will appoint one. If you cannot afford one, the state will provide a Public Defender."

Constance stood before the judge, her eyes downcast. Taking a deep breath, she raised her head and began to speak when a commotion in the gallery interrupted the proceedings.

"Permission to address the bench, your Honor!"

"Order in the court!" Judge Lester banged her gavel with relish. In all her years presiding over night court, she had never before had the chance to use her gavel. She banged it again for good measure. "Order in the court. This is all highly irregular. Who is requesting to address me? Do you represent the defendant?"

"I do, your Honor."

"But I don't have a lawyer," Constance Carruthers exclaimed, looking over her shoulder where, to her surprise, she saw Daisy MacDailey wearing violet and gold muumuu festooned with giant orchids. Standing next to her was a brown-haired man with severe eyebrows over penetrating brown eyes, wearing a Savile Row suit of grey worsted wool, bench made burgundy brogues, a single needle pink oxford shirt and a purple Hermes tie.

"Excuse me, your Honor, but I have been retained to represent Ms. Carruthers." Ken Ruby's rich baritone resonated in the almost empty courtroom.

"Mr. Ruby, the court recognizes you. You may step forward. And may I say it's quite a surprise to find you here." Judge Lester peered through her thick lenses. "I'm more accustomed to seeing you on the 6 o'clock news."

Ken Ruby was often seen on the local news shows. He was the first choice for high-profile criminal cases – Johhny Depp, Kyle Rittenhouse and former President Donald Trump were some of his recent clients.

"Your flattery is appreciated, Judge Lester. But I'm just a simple country lawyer, compelled to help those who face injustice. In this matter, it's Ms. MacDailey who has enlisted my services."

"Daisy MacDailey – in my courtroom! Well, this is an unusual night. Two celebrities and a murder case. Well, councilor, do you have any motions to make?"

"Yes, your Honor. I would like to move for an adjournment of this arraignment until I have the opportunity to review the charges with the district attorney. I would also like to request the immediate release of my client pending further proceedings."

"Highly irregular. Do you expect me to waive bail and release the defendant on her own recognizance?"

"No, your Honor. We are prepared to post up to one million dollars bail."

"That's a lot of money, Mr. Ruby. From where would funds be obtained?"

"If I may, your Honor?" Daisy MacDailey spoke in her most delicate voice.

"Yes, Ms. MacDailey?"

"I am willing to post my home at 55 Sutton Place in lieu of one million dollars bail. I am also proposing that Ms. Carruthers be remanded to house arrest in my apartment for the duration of these proceedings."

"That's a very generous offer, Ms. MacDailey."

"Constance Carruthers has been a valued employee for ten years, your Honor. I feel compelled to support her during this terrible ordeal."

"I see. And what does the defendant have to say?"

Constance Carruthers looked at Daisy. She had never heard her speak so quietly, or look so gentle. Ken Ruby leaned over and whispered a few words in her ear. Constance looked up at Judge Lester. "Your Honor, if the court accepts this offer, I am willing to abide by any constraints which may be ordered."

"Very well. Mr. Ruby, motion granted. The court releases the defendant into the custody of Daisy MacDailey and accepts the property at 55 Sutton Place in lieu of $1,000,000 bail. The defendant is dismissed pending the rescheduling of her arraignment. You're released for now, Ms. Carruthers."

Daisy ran over to Constance, wrapping her ample arm around her shoulder. "Connie, you were so brave! I'm so proud of you. Now let's go get you cleaned up. I'm sure you'd love a shower."

"Well, Ms. MacDailey, I don't know what ..."

"You don't need to know nothing but that I'll take care of you," Daisy said as she took CC's arm. "And don't worry about this murder thing. Kenny here is a genius. He'll get the charges reduced to manslaughter ..."

"Involuntary manslaughter. Then we'll plea bargain to reckless endangerment. With luck, you'll end up with probation."

"I'm not paying for fucking luck."

The well-heeled lawyer hailed a cab. "I'll let you know how things go with the DA."

"Bust the old bastard's balls for me. Now, let's get the hell out of here." Daisy squeezed her orchid-draped frame into the cab, pulling CC in along with her. "You know, Connie, you look great in orange. You should wear it more often.

32

"Zack! Turn on the television! Quick!"

It was Mayor Mike.

"...sad events of a week ago. It's always sad when the City of New York loses an artist, especially one so young and vital as Ms. Mildow. And it's always sad when the city loses an arts institution. So today we mourn the passing of The Marxist Sisters as well as their talented director. And though we may have tears in our eyes, we must not succumb to our grief. We must look to the future, carry forward the dreams that were embodied here at the Courtyard Playhouse. And so it is a great pleasure to take this grave moment to announce that on this site, Big Bush Stratagems has agreed to erect the Teena Towers Condominium Complex and International Institute for Contemporary Dramaturgy."

Zach nearly dropped the bowl of cherries he was preparing. "Did you hear that?"

Jaq came running down the stairs. "Yes! Can you believe it?"

"Thank you, thank you, Bushwick." The Mayor's adenoids sounded even squeakier on TV. "At this time, it's an honor for me to introduce a young lady who embodies the best of New York. A young woman who came here to follow her dreams, a young woman who labored unstintingly, working long hours in difficult conditions, a young woman who represents the indomitable spirit of this great city of ours. Ladies and gentlemen, with great pleasure I present to you the founding director of the International Institute for Contemporary Dramaturgy, Ms. Sioban Koslowski."

"Shy!" Jaq exclaimed.

"That girl knows how to land on her feet," Zach said admiringly.

"Thank you, Mr. Mayor." Her red hair gleaming in the Brooklyn sun, her bandages still visible, Shy Koslowski stepped to the microphone. "It's hard for me to believe that just a few months ago, I was new in town, a recent college graduate looking for a break, while today I'm standing beside the Mayor of the City of New York, director of an organization that is destined to make an important contribution to the illustrious history of the New York theater. And while the events that brought me to this juncture are fraught with sorrow, they will be a constant incentive to demand of myself a complete commitment to my position as director of the International Institute for Contemporary Dramaturgy."

"She speaks pretty well for a kid," Zach was stirring some pulverized Ritalin into the cherries.

"Don't condescend. She's a college graduate, which is something you can't say."

The cheers faded on the TV as Shy continued. "And as director, I'd like to take this moment to announce the Institute's inaugural project, a collaboration with the Wild Petunias, Ithaca's only gay theater company, on their upcoming production of 'The Boys From Syracuse.'"

"Can't wait for that."

"Shut up, Zach."

"In closing, I want to say thank you to two people without whom I wouldn't be standing here today, who gave me the strength to keep going, who literally saved

107

my life. Zach Mack, Piemaker to the Stars, and Jaq Mack were there for me when I needed them the most and I can never thank them enough for that."

"Oh, how sweet."

"I'll name a pie after you, kiddo."

"And I can't leave without a big shoutout to the most wonderful cat in the world, Pieface O'Riley!"

"Did you hear that? You're famous, Pieface."

"Mer-ee-owl"

"I don't think he's impressed," Zach said as he flipped off the TV.

"Zach, you can be such a noodge. What are you working on, anyway?"

"Just playing around with a new idea. I think I'll call it The Dramaturge's Delight."

"Come on, it's Shy's pie, give her the credit! Do you think she'll like it?"

"She will if she likes chocolate. And uppers."

"Hey, what happened to the cocoanut custard?"

"Never got around to finishing it. Once they cancelled the opening, there was no point. But to the baker, go the spoils."

"What does that mean?"

"It means we have an eightball of Peru's finest. It's in the kitchen. Want some?"

"One of these days, you're going to get yourself in trouble, Mr. Mack."

"I'll just blame it on Pieface. Say I was under the influence of an evil famil-iar."

"Pieface won't like that."

"So what? The cat will mew."

From the kitchen came the unmistakable sound of breaking glass.

"That sounded bad. You better go check it out, Zach."

Zach Mack, still stirring the bowl of cherries, walked to the kitchen. There, perched on the counter, was a small black cat with greenish-yellow eyes and a bright red tongue looking at a pile of mirror shards and 100% pure Peruvian flake cocaine lying on the floor.

"PIEFACE!"

SHY'S PIE

For the cherries

        1 cup fresh sour cherries

        ¼ cup kirshwasser

        ½ cup superfine sugar

        15 10mg Ritalin, powderized

For the crust

        1 cup shelled walnuts

        ½ cup bleached flour

        dash salt

        ½ cup butter

For the mousse –

        6 eggs separated

        12oz. 70% cocoa dark chocolate

For the topping

        ½ cup heavy cream

        1 tsp vanilla

        splash kirshwasser

        ¼ cup superfine sugar

        shaved dark chocolate

        chopped walnuts

Clean and pit cherries. Combine sugar and Ritalin, add to kirshwasser. Soak cherries in liquid 4 days.

Place walnuts on baking sheet and roast in 325' oven five minutes. When cool, grind very fine. Combine flour, salt and ground nuts. Cut in butter. Form into a ball and chill well. Roll out dough. Place in deepdish pie plate. Line with parchment paper, protect edge with foil. Bake in 400' oven 5 minutes. Remove foil and paper, bake till crust just begins to color. Cool on wire rack.

Melt chocolate in double boiler. Stir in yolks and remove from heat. Beat eggwhites till stiff peaks form. Carefully fold chocolate mixture into beaten whites, stirring gently till blended. Stir cherries into mousse, reserving a dozen or so for topping. Turn into baked shell.

Whip cream till soft peaks form. Add vanilla and kirshwasser. Slowly add sugar while beating cream till stiff. Transfer to pastry bag. Top of pie with cream rosettes. Dot with remaining cherries. Cover with shaved chocolate. Sprinkle with chopped walnuts. Chill well.

Serves 4-8

E Penniman James lives and writes in Brooklyn, NY. His poetry chapbooks, *Two Poem Cycles* and *3rd Person*, (AlienBuddha Press), are available on Amazon. His poems also appear in the print anthologies *Birds Fall Silent in the Mechanical Sea* and *The Shape Made by a Curve* (great weather for Media 2020 and 2023), *Brownstone Poets 2023 Anthology*, *Pluto 1* (Propoetsy, 2022), and *Lyrics of Mature Hearts* (Gordon Bois Publications, 2020) as well as a number of online and print publications.